FOWL PLAY

A Magical Romantic Comedy (with a body count)

RJ BLAIN

Fowl Play
A Magical Romantic Comedy (with a body count)
RJ Blain

Warning: This novella contains humor, romance, magic, puns, bodies, and a short detour from reality. No plots were harmed in the making of this story.

Instead of a quiet dance retreat where she could escape the insanity of being the daughter of an angel, a succubus, and a lycanthrope, Emma Sansaul plummets into the middle of murder, mayhem, and mischief. As becoming the next victim of a crazed serial killer is not on her itinerary, she's left with no choice but to join forces with Agent Kenneth Bernard to find the murderer, the one man on Earth capable of making her hissing mad one second and in need of a cold shower the next.

Cover Design by Rebecca Frank of Bewitching Book Covers

ONE

What have I told you about bringing random incubi home?

NORMAL PEOPLE worried about delays at the airport, dealing with security, and other travel snarls when heading off on an adventure. Me?

One of my mothers was a succubus, and she'd brought home an incubus for me to enjoy. Like all his demonic kin, he was a dark beauty oozing sin with a dash of temptation, offering everything a girl could want and more. If I didn't get the hell out of Dodge, I'd miss my flight, lose my virginity, and discover the joys of having an on-call incubus.

Heaven help me.

"No, Mom." I pointed at the incubus, whose grin promised the immediate disintegration of my panties if I let him get anywhere near me. "What have I told you about bringing random incubi home?"

"You keep telling me not to do it like you actually get a say in the matter. This is my house, young lady. And in my house, I'll bring home company whenever I want."

Why, why, why did I have an angel for a mother, a

succubus for a mother, and a bloody, feather-brained lycan-thrope for a father? I thought a little screaming was warranted, so I started with my father. "Dad!? Mom brought home an incubus again."

"Talk to your other mother, Emma," my father yelled back from across the house. "I'm busy with the chicks right now."

Damned feather-brained, chicken-obsessed idiot of a swan!

"Language!" Ma ordered from up the stairs, proving I had an unwanted snoop poking around in my thoughts again.

"Ma, Mom's going to make me late for the airport. Can you please deal with this situation?"

"You're still dressed, he's not influencing you, and despite your current belief, he won't actually disintegrate your panties. Stop being such a baby. Maybe if you wouldn't run every time your mom brought home a guest, she wouldn't find it so amusing to bring guests home with her."

"You're a fallen angel, aren't you? There's no other expla-nation." I bowed my head, wondered how I'd make the thirty feet to my car without being ambushed, further delayed, or otherwise blocked from going to Boulder, Colorado to prac-tice dancing and escape from the monotony of set perfor-mances at the theater.

"No, I'm just fair, and for once in her life, your mom hasn't done anything wrong."

"Yet! She hasn't done anything wrong yet."

"Louisa, perhaps you should take your pet incubus home. You know how cranky George gets when you bring home an incubus for Emma. Can we go one day without having an incident in this house, please?"

Mom scowled, lashing her tail and clamping her wings

close to her back. "Damn it! I went through a lot of effort to catch this one."

Once my mothers started going at it, nothing short of divine intervention would stop them. Mouthing an apology to the bemused incubus, I snatched my luggage and retreated out the front door.

Some days, living with telepaths and empaths annoyed the hell out of me, but once they started duking it out in the privacy of their thoughts, the world could end without either one noticing.

"Have a safe flight, Miss Emma." The incubus held the front door open for me. "The combination for the lock on your steering wheel is 4-2-7-1."

"I don't have a clue who you are, but you're now my friend."

"Call me Rafil."

"Like Israfil?" Having met the archangel, if he ever found out there was a cheeky incubus edging in on his turf, it'd get ugly. With my luck, it'd happen in my house, as my mothers had no shame and enjoyed their power plays as much as my father enjoyed watching them.

I'd been born into a family of raving lunatics.

The incubus's grin confirmed my fears. "I live to yank his chain. It keeps him on his toes. If you change your mind and want to play with me, give me a call. I'd be glad to introduce you to the true pleasures of life."

I bolted for my car like the devil himself was hot on my heels. I contemplated murdering Mom when I saw the chain wrapped around my steering wheel, which ran out the window to loop through my rim, ensuring I wouldn't be going anywhere without the combination. The number worked. I dumped the mess on the lawn for my mom to clean up, shoved my bags into the backseat, and bailed before my parents could stop me.

Had I been on an international flight, I would've missed it by a mile, but fortune smiled on me for a rare change, and I squeaked through security with minutes to spare. Until I was safely on board, I wouldn't test my luck. I couldn't afford to. Ma could teleport, and nobody with half a brain stopped an angel on a mission.

No matter what, I needed to catch my flight. Once on board, Ma wouldn't interfere with the plane; it went against the household rules. It only took one plane crash, and I still had no idea how no one had died in that crash, myself included.

I blamed angelic magic, which was likely why my ma had escaped with a 'minor' fine.

Airplanes weren't cheap, a lesson I'd learned when the bill arrived for its replacement. It was so not cheap I'd fainted when I'd seen the invoice with my name on it.

With a little help from Dad, I'd expanded the rules to apply to boats, cars, and other vehicles, giving me good odds of arriving at my destination alive.

I made it to the gate with a minute to spare, and before the attendant could glare at me, I babbled profuse apologies and held out my boarding pass. Unless I was an inch from death, I'd learned not to pray for anything.

Fortunately for me, prayer wasn't needed, and she waved me through the gate to the boarding ramp.

Everyone stared at me while I hauled my carryon to the back of the plane, the cheapest seat I could get.

Had I known I'd be seated beside Kenneth Bernard, I would've accepted the incubus's invitation, missed the dance retreat altogether, and liked it. I would've even marched into my father's office, informing him I'd love to be his partner in his law practice, ensuring a substantial raise and far better job security.

Embarrassment often led to me doing foolish things, as did Mom. The first time I'd met Kenneth, I'd been riding a pixie dust high so intense it'd taken three rounds of neutralizer to bring me down, a stunt that'd landed me in solitary for a night. I'd escaped without being charged, as I'd been smart enough to request an angel confirm that I hadn't known the pixie dust was an illegal grade, but the embarrassment remained.

"Hey, jail bird. Fancy meeting you here," he greeted me with his cockiest grin. "I saved you a seat."

In a move meant to remind me I'd be trapped with him for the next three hours, he patted the cushion beside him.

To keep the stewardess from murdering me, I wasted no time shoving my bag in the last spot in the overhead bin. I cursed the day I'd been talked into going to a bar with Mom. Only Mom would hook me up with illegal pixie dust and use it as a chance to teach me about the realities of life.

I blamed Ma for blindly trusting Mom, resulting in my arrest that night. Then again, I suspected Ma had known Mom had been planning *something* to get me in trouble. Both of my mothers believed that important life lessons needed to be learned through experience.

Worse, I was willing to bet Mom had gone out of her way to pick Kenneth as the one to bust me. He was her type, and I'd learned early on I was my mother's daughter as much as I was my father's. Most days, I considered myself confused, attracted to the exact wrong sort of man. In my case, I harbored an unfortunate interest in the muscle-bound cop with an intense dislike for narcotics incapable of tolerating anyone with a wandering eye.

Ma and Dad took the blame for that, although Mom smiled, shrugged, and accepted her share of guilt over how I'd turned out.

With no other choice, I took my seat, buckled up, and bowed my head. "No one warned me this was a cop-infested flight," I complained.

"Please, jail bird. I'm in the FBI. I'm too amazing to just be a cop."

"Amazing? Seriously? You busted me on pixie dust," I muttered.

"It's a pretty amazing day when I get to bust someone for using a legal substance in an illegal fashion. For future reference, you're not supposed to inhale pixie dust. I recommend ingesting it in a good drink. Stick to the legal grades. I could've had you licking out of my hand on command. Also, avoid keeping company with succubi. I should've suggested that first."

"That succubus is my mother, Kenneth."

He stared at me, both brows lifted high. "You don't look like a succubus."

"My other mother is an angel."

"No wonder you went wild. First night on the town without your angelic mother watching you like a hawk?" Kenneth's smirk drove me crazy, and I wasn't sure if I wanted to slap it off his face or test the claim that the lycanthropy virus couldn't be spread through a little tongue-on-tongue action.

It wasn't fair my nightmare in the flesh could give an incubus a run for his money.

"No, I was just an idiot for letting Mom talk me into going to the bar with her." I shrugged. "After the first three drinks, who cared if sniffing pixie dust wasn't conventional usage?"

"I knew I should've written up the succubus for possession, too."

"We both know she dumped the entire stash on me so she could laugh at me while I experienced arrest. She called it a 'learning experience.'"

"Well, I can't say she's wrong. You did learn something, right?"

"Yes, I did. I learned I have an allergy to being arrested by egotistical cops who don't wear uniforms and hang out at bars on a Tuesday night."

He dared to laugh, and I wondered how I'd make it through the rest of the flight with my sanity intact.

TWO

Angels preferred purer humans.

ONE DAY, I needed to ask my mothers why I'd drawn the short straw of life when I contracted the lycanthropy virus from my father while still in the womb. The how of it made sense; my father loved both of my mothers, and the only way to ensnare a succubus was to keep her busy in bed or eternally pregnant.

I suspected Dad would've helped double the swan lycanthrope population had my mothers cooperated with him. To be fair, it wouldn't be hard for him.

Swans came few and far between, and they only showed up courtesy of a magical hot spot. He'd already doubled the population once having me. That interested the CDC, as until I'd been born, they hadn't thought angelic children could contract the lycanthropy virus in the womb.

There was a first for everything, and I thanked Ma every day I hadn't been recruited to be a CDC research subject. If they could figure out why I'd contracted lycanthropy, they might be able to figure out more about how the virus spread between species. They also wanted to know why my virus levels remained low. It'd take a lot of effort on my part to infect someone. By their estimate, I'd have to give either a full blood donation or spend at least a week seducing my partner to have even a chance of passing on my special brand of lunacy.

I blamed His contribution to my existence, which had likely manipulated the DNA from my mothers, thus allowing my father's DNA to hold a slight majority. Then again, who knew? I was the only documented case of an angel, a succubus, and a lycanthrope hooking up and having a child.

Angels preferred purer humans.

"That's a pretty serious expression you're rocking," Kenneth said, nudging me with his elbow. "What's got your feathers in a kink?"

In all my meetings with Kenneth, I'd learned a few important rules of engagement. The man lived to tease me, and he loved nothing more than when I fluffed my feathers and got riled up by his comments. Playing it cool, in turn, drove him wild, and I enjoyed turning the tables on him. If he wanted a talk, I'd give him one.

Maybe the shock would make him faint, resulting in a quiet, peaceful flight to Colorado.

"How do you feel about lycanthropes?"

"I work in the narcotics field. I run into them almost every day. You'd be surprised at the number of lycanthropes who'll try illegal drugs hoping to cure themselves of the virus. It's a shame, really. For something incurable, it comes with a lot of benefits. I don't understand why someone would risk their health trying to get rid of a virus that prolongs their life."

"It's the lack of job opportunities and generalized fear.

People get nasty towards lycanthropes on a bad day and run away on a good one."

"Spoken like someone who'd know. Who do you know that's a lycanthrope?"

I pointed at myself. "A gift from Dad."

"Didn't you say your mother's that succubus who got your arrested, jail bird?"

"She did it to piss Ma off and teach me a few lessons about life. I'm convinced of it."

Kenneth's expression went blank. "Your mother did it to piss your ma off?"

His tone conveyed a mountain of questions, and I relaxed in my seat, wishing I could stretch my legs. By the time the plane landed, I'd be cramped from head to toe and likely require an intervention to keep from falling on my ass the instant I tried to stand up. "Yep."

"You're the daughter of a triad."

Triad? That was a nice way to label the convoluted three-some required for an angel to have a child with a human. "I haven't heard it put that way before. Interesting."

"You're part angel."

"I'm a little bit of heaven, a little bit of hell, and a whole lot of lycanthrope."

"I never would've guessed."

"That's the general idea."

"Contagious?"

"If you're hoping to arrest me again, you're going to be sorely disappointed." I smirked, reaching down so I could retrieve my wallet from my purse between my feet, and dug out the handy little CDC-issued card displaying my lycan-thropy infection status. I offered it to him. "They made this for me because I'm special, and they didn't want to figure out how to add this shit to my driver's license."

His brows rose as he read the information on the card, which included risk of transmission through intercourse, defined to a number of instances, and how much blood it would take for infection to occur. "Most women would not be happy to have this information put on a card they're required to show law enforcement if asked."

"It's a badge of pride. If a man wants my virus, he'll have to earn it."

"This number is defined within a set number of hours, jail bird."

"He'll really have to want it and work to earn it." I grinned, snatched my card out of his hand, and waved it in his face. "I don't take chances, but this is my free pass to do so if I wanted. I just have to show my partner the card and be willing to face Ma's wrath."

"It must be pretty easy to get angelic verification when your mother's an angel."

"Well, one of them. The other? She's totally the type to get her daughter arrested because she can't play with the local law enforcement anymore."

Kenneth's eyes narrowed. "I'm not sure I want to ask."

"That's probably wise. My father is a lycanthrope, and you know how they get."

"Jealously possessive with a single partner."

"Well, Dad has two partners, and he's jealously possessive over both of them. Mom tried to escape once just to see what Dad would do. He dragged her back home by her tail. Had I not been six and impressionable, I'm sure he would've chained her in the basement."

"You lead an even more interesting life than I ever could

have imagined, and I feel a little bad I interfered with your high. After dealing with that sort of thing, I'd want to get a hit of pixie dust, too. Next time, use legal vendors."

"I had no idea it wasn't legal, damn it!"

"You also curse a lot more than I expected from the child of an angel."

Growing up, I'd faced the expectations of the general public; children of angels were supposed to be faultless beings, good-natured and pure without exception. People were stupid.

Had I not been infected with lycanthropy from before birth, I would've been a human like any other. The mix of genetics didn't instill any sort of morality on people in my shoes.

That was all part of being human.

No matter how many times I'd ask Ma, the answer had been the same. He let us make our own mistakes, which we'd pay for in the afterlife. I got the feeling He would rather enforce law and order on the universe so he wouldn't have to deal with sorting souls, but He kept His word, and that meant humans retained the free will to screw up their lives.

I was a big fan of having the freedom to fuck up my life at my whim.

"You're also a lot quieter on a flight than I anticipated. The baby in the front row is making more of a fuss than you are."

I blinked, canting my head to listen. "There's a baby in the front row?"

"Exactly. She cried a bit before you boarded. I think she thought we'd be late because someone couldn't get to the gate in a timely fashion."

It amused me Kenneth thought a baby had the ability to

judge if a plane was delayed from taking off due to a slightly late passenger. I let him hold onto that belief.

"It's Mom's fault. She brought an incubus home and chained my steering wheel because she hates when I leave home. The only reason I escaped the house was because Ma picked a fight with Mom. I bet the incubus and Dad will end up having some beers and lamenting their lot in life. I'm seriously considering running for the border."

"You still live with your parents?"

I scowled at the laughter in his voice. "You try being the daughter of a succubus, an angel, and a lycanthrope sometime. The last time I tried to move out, it was mass hysterics."

The rent was a lot cheaper, too. Even with Dad gouging me on my share of the mortgage, I wouldn't have been able to afford living in a nice neighborhood otherwise unless I joined his practice and put my expensive degree to good use.

Maintaining my license through mandatory pro bono hours and continued education courses kept him happy and kept his hopes up that I'd join the firm someday.

Until then, I pretended I wasn't over-educated for an understudy dancer.

"I have a hard time believing your story. Why would there be mass hysterics?"

I held up a finger. "I dance for a living."

Kenneth clamped his lips together in a valiant effort to keep from laughing. I'd seen my father do the exact same thing enough times to know he'd taken a long walk off a short pier directly into a sea of perversion. Men.

"Ballet, thank you."

"Go on. Continue, please." His voice wavered from his effort to contain his mirth.

I held up a second finger. "Mom worries, as she believes

I'm helpless. She's convinced every single predator on the planet will lock on and come after me the instant I leave the house."

"This explains why she brought home an incubus and chained your steering wheel. However, most parents would consider an incubus to be a predator."

"But the incubus would be an approved predator."

"And your father?"

"He's a lycanthrope. What do you think?"

"A battle to near-death to determine if the man after his daughter meets his approval," Kenneth replied, and his laughter finally slipped out. "I'm really curious now. How did mass hysteria take hold on your triad of parents?"

"Ma crashed a plane trying to retrieve me because Mom cried and Dad paced holes in the floor. We had to implement a ban on any of my parents teleporting into vehicles, especially moving ones, to retrieve me. This rule is only waived if I'm at actual risk of death and not just trying to escape the insanity that is my life."

Kenneth's expression turned neutral. "Your Ma crashed a plane. You're seriously telling me an angel managed to crash a plane?"

"I got billed for the entire replacement cost of the plane. It was awful. Ma paid for it, and I, to this day, do not know where she got the money. I'm not entirely convinced she didn't rob a bank. No one would ever suspect an angel of robbing a bank." I shrugged. "I've been informed I shouldn't take up bank robbery as a career."

"Considering how poorly your foray into illegal substances went, I second that advice. You'd be a terrible bank robber."

Any other day, Kenneth would've annoyed me, but I

recognized the truth when it smacked me in the face. "Yeah. Mom's teaching method was very effective. Jail is not for me."

"You'd be surprised how many people habitually get arrested to serve jail time."

"Free meals, free board, and good health care?"

"Bingo. It became a serious enough problem where the government required an overhaul of the prison system to stop inmates from draining the system trying to get out of the daily responsibilities of life. That's why community service is heavily on the rise and long-term prison time is reserved for severe crimes; if an angel verifies the motive was to stay in prison, those individuals are moved to a housing unit and forced to work full-time community service in exchange for a stipend and medical services."

I reminded myself that law-enforcement types lived and breathed everything to do with the judiciary system. I could handle listening to Kenneth chat my ear off for a few hours. It wouldn't kill me to pretend I was learning something new.

Probably.

"And had I been actually guilty of willfully snorting up high-grade pixie dust?"

"Rehab, some community service, and a light slap on the wrist to go with your overnight detention. You'd probably be assigned someone in law enforcement to keep an eye on your activities to see if the rehab worked."

"That seems like an expensive way to deal with someone who just wants to be happy."

"That grade of dust circumvents your free will, jail bird. You could've become someone's slave. There's a reason you were put in solitary until the neutralizer worked."

"All three doses of it," I grumbled.

"That was unusual. But, most people don't snort the dust. It was an educational evening for me, a very amusing, educational evening."

How delightful. I amused the man who'd busted me. "I learned my lesson."

"Which one? There's so many you might've learned from this incident. I lost count."

"You're a sadistic bastard."

He laughed. "It's one of my charms. Sorry. It's been a long week at work, and I'm looking forward to a chance to unwind for the weekend."

"Are you catching a connecting flight out of Colorado, then?"

"No, I'm going to Colorado."

"To unwind for the weekend?"

"That's the idea. It's a nice, quiet place. I'm going to a resort outside of Boulder."

Alarm bells blared through my head. While Boulder did have resorts, I hadn't really thought of the place as a mecca of resorts, which put me at high risk of being at the same resort as Kenneth. "You're going to a resort in Boulder for the weekend?"

"Well, it's more like a week. I was told I needed to take time off, and if I didn't, I'd be put on mandatory leave. My boss gave me a list of acceptable activities, as he thought I'd need help picking something appropriate."

"Your boss sent you to Boulder for a week-long stay at a resort?"

"And he's making me pay for it, too, the jackass."

I had so many questions and hardly knew where to begin unraveling the mystery seated beside me. "Did you do something to piss him off?"

"I think so. What, I'm not sure. My work performance has been really good. He gave me a week's notice to wrap up my current work, told me I was going out of town for the week, and that he wasn't accepting no for an answer."

"Is that even legal?"

Kenneth shrugged. "Hell if I know."

"At least he let you pick from a list of options, I guess. Did he plan your entire vacation?"

"I'm pretty sure he did. He told me if I left without an itinerary, I'd get bored and wander home, then I'd end up going back to work because I have no life."

"That explains why you were at a quiet bar on a Tuesday night." I wrinkled my nose. "I have the worst luck."

"You have fantastic luck. You were arrested by me, and there's something to be said for being arrested by the best."

Between Ma, Mom, and Dad, I got my daily fill of egos. As killing Kenneth and tossing him out of the plane would land me in prison and make me miss my retreat, I did my best to pretend he wasn't a pretty annoyance. "Did you hit your head this morning getting out of bed?"

"Not nice," he complained.

"Well, there are treatments for concussions and delusions. It's important to find out what sort of medication you need. Is your boss aware of this? You should probably tell him. Then he would've had you spending your money on treatments rather than taking a flight to Colorado to stay at a resort."

"Do you have a master's degree in sarcasm? Obviously, I need to be taking lessons from you."

"As murder is on the list of things I'm not allowed to do unless I'm about to be murdered, I have to hope my sarcastic wit kills you. Unfortunately, I'm concerned you'll just like it."

He laughed, proving me right. "Why are you flying to Colorado?"

"Work." Technically, it was as much play as it was work, but he didn't need to know that.

"You have a performance?"

"Not quite. I don't perform again for another two weeks; I was overdue for some time off, too." I shifted in my seat to try to stretch my cramping calves. "Keeping in shape and honing my skills is an important part of work. Staying fit for performances doesn't just magically happen."

Kenneth's grin worried me, and he pulled out a folded piece of paper out of his wallet. "I just love being the bearer of good news."

Crap. I eyed the paper warily. "How is a piece of paper from a copper good news?"

"Please, jail bird. I'm not just some copper. I'm an FBI agent. I'm a high-class law enforcement officer."

I glared at him. "What's that paper?"

"It's my itinerary, prepared by my boss to get me out of his hair for a while."

I rolled my eyes but took the sheet out of his hand, unfolded it, and looked over it. Official FBI letterhead supported his claim he'd been subjected to a mandatory vacation at his boss's insistence, as did the terse opening lines informing Kenneth he'd stick to his itinerary or he'd be subjected to hell shifts for the next year. "Your boss is an ass."

"He means well, and he gets tired of trying to explain to his boss why I don't take time off."

I snorted and resumed reading the list of activities, which included the flight, landing in Colorado, and the confirmation of my fears; Kenneth and I would be at the same resort for the entire time.

Had I been wise, I would've invited the incubus to be my dance partner. At least that way, I knew exactly what to expect from the living, breathing sex machine on a mission to get laid.

Kenneth, as always, remained a mystery, and I had no idea what being stuck with him for a week would do for my peace of mind.

If he looked as good shirtless as he did in a shirt, I'd be in real trouble, and the men in the dance field often wore form-fitting outfits, which showed off their assets.

Was I supposed to pray for help, offer my thanks, or run away? I'd find out soon enough.

KENNETH TOOK advantage of our shared destination to coerce me into taking a cab with him to the resort. I hated money. Money made me do stupid things. Had money not been an issue, I would've rejected his offer to split the bill.

At least he hadn't offered to pay the whole thing. I would've protested on principle. Of all the traits I'd inherited from Ma, my inability to let go of keeping things as fair as possible annoyed the hell out of me some days.

Mom thought it was funny and sometimes questioned if I was actually her child, and she did it because she knew it annoyed Ma.

"See? This trip is already looking up. We both saved money on the cab. It's a mutually beneficial arrangement."

Why couldn't my father have been a wolf rather than the world's first swan? Growling intimidated people.

Honking?

Honking induced fits of laughter.

Unfortunately, swans were assholes, had an aggression streak a mile wide, and when shifted, my father weighed in at almost seventy pounds, which was a lot of swan. Only an idiot screwed around with a mundane swan. Dad could break bones without thinking about it, and his beak could cut through skin with ease. If he wanted, he could gouge a hole in someone's throat with a single strike. Pretty and feathered didn't mean helpless. Once I shifted, assuming it ever happened, I'd be able to fly without the help of an airplane.

Dad thought once I settled down and found a man for myself, my virus would replicate so I could get on with providing him grandchicks to spoil. I found it funny he advised me against claiming an angel and an incubus for myself, as it would limit his ability to spoil high numbers of grandchicks.

"Jail bird?"

"I'm trying to figure out how this happened," I muttered, slumping in my seat. "I must be cursed."

"Saving money on cab fare is never a bad thing. Come on. You have to admit it could be a lot worse. Despite appearances, I do know how to dance."

Kenneth could dance? I narrowed my eyes. "What style?"

"I started with swing dancing, but I like variety. That's why my boss had this place on the list. I fill in sometimes in dance classes for people without a partner, and he's had to call me out of class a few times to deal with cases."

Trouble had a name: Kenneth. If I could forget about the whole being arrested thing, he counted as the rare unicorn ripe for the picking. He kept in shape, he had a nice face, he could string multiple words together resulting in a coherent sentence, and he could dance.

If Mom found out, mass hysteria would begin again, and she'd be gunning for me to stake some claims on him, Ma would be determined to marry me off, and Dad would beat Kenneth within an inch of his life. While I had certain issues involving being arrested and assigned a sadly accurate nickname, Kenneth didn't deserve exposure to my family.

"Never, ever tell my mother you can dance. Either one of them."

"Why not?" Kenneth's eyes widened. "Do they dislike dancers?"

"The exact opposite. Don't ask what Mom would do, Ma would be planning a wedding, and Dad would find some way to murder you without earning Ma's ire."

"Should I be concerned?"

"Only if they find out you can dance. For a lycanthrope, Dad's not too bad. Usually. Unless anyone looks at either of my mothers or me. After that, all bets are off. Consider yourself fortunate Dad isn't part of a pack."

"That depends. Who would the pack be helping, assuming he was part of a pack?"

"Probably my mothers. It'd be a disaster."

Either foolishly brave or he simply didn't care, Kenneth laughed. "I'll take my chances. How bad could it be? One of your mothers is an angel."

The poor, deluded fool. "Just don't come crying to me later."

"I'll keep that in mind."

THREE

Hell was sharing a room with Kenneth Bernard.

After dealing with my parents and a flight with Kenneth, I wanted nothing more than to stagger to my room and collapse on to the bed, but fate, the devil, and maybe even the heavens conspired against me.

Somehow, my room had been double booked, and the asshole who'd booked in after me had gotten to it first, leaving me up shit creek without a paddle, boat, or option of a new room, as the resort had nothing available.

I'd have to book something in Boulder twenty minutes away if I wanted to attend the retreat. Getting a rental hadn't been in my budget, and neither had paying for a cab for so many trips. When the going got tough, the tough kicked ass, but I wanted to crawl to a corner and cry. If I had to call home to bum money from Ma, I'd never hear the end of it.

"What's wrong?" Kenneth asked, propping his elbows on the desk beside me. "You look like you're about to give up. The last time I saw that expression on your face, I was helping you into the cab."

"They double booked my room, and they don't have anything else available," I confessed. Lying wouldn't do any good; he'd figure it out right away or decide to do some investigating to discover the truth.

"Seriously?"

"A computer glitch, or so it seems. My reservation looks correct, she even says it does, but someone else is in the room. I'd even booked first. This is a disaster. I'll have to get a room in fucking Boulder."

"My room has two beds. Staying in Boulder is ridiculous. I don't mind if you share with me."

Hell was sharing a room with Kenneth Bernard. It was heaven, too, a heaven I'd indulge in once he went to sleep. I could watch him without any guilt. Good looks, bad luck, and an idiotic determination to stay at the retreat left me with one choice: I'd share a room with my new best friend for life, and I'd choke showing him the proper gratitude for saving my ass. "I can pay for half the room," I mumbled.

"We'll worry about it after we get home."

I bowed my head, sighed, and regretted the day I thought I'd like going to Colorado for a dance retreat. "Thanks."

"Please add her to my room," Kenneth demanded. He pulled his reservation out of his pocket and handed it over. "I trust this won't be a problem?"

"Of course not, Mr. Bernard. That's very generous of you."

"She's a friend."

Any other day, I would've considered his claim a stretch. He'd be my best friend for my bailing my ass out, at least until after the retreat ended. Staying with him beat calling Ma and begging for help because of a double booking. If I had to call Ma, I worried all three of my parents would show up.

If all three of my parents showed up and found out about Kenneth's offer, he might end up a friend with permanent benefits.

I'd have to be really careful when Dad called in to check in on me. If I gave any indication I was sharing a room with a man, Ma would show up, as there'd been nothing in the household rules barring her from popping into hotel rooms to check in on me.

Mom would just hand me every single birth control method she could get her hands on, some for him, some for me, and instructions on how to keep him in bed long enough to infect him with my virus.

I hoped Kenneth wouldn't mind if I locked myself in the bathroom, took a long soak, and hid for a while.

Within five minutes, we were on route to the elevator, and I found some comfort in the realization my week couldn't get much worse. I waited until we were inside to say, "Thanks. I do really appreciate it."

"I've been in your shoes before; double bookings are the worst. And to add insult to injury? The time it happened to me? Some bigwig with more money than sense wanted my room and paid the hotel off to get what he wanted. They didn't have a new room for me, either, and I ultimately forced them to pay for my room at a rival hotel, as I'd recorded that the hotel had been paid off to 'accidentally' double book my room. After a silent presentation of my badge, they were eager to compensate me."

I liked that Kenneth played dirty with hotel management, but I wondered what sort of room he'd booked that a bigwig coveted it. "It sounds like you have interesting travel adventures."

"It's part of my job. Sometimes I'll go undercover for a big bust, and I need to stay in the right sort of accommodations to get the right sort of attention. Depending on what's happening, I've even hired escorts to keep me company for a week so I could flush a dealer out. Those jobs are always interesting."

I arched a brow. "Your job literally involves hiring sex workers to catch drug dealers?"

"I don't sleep with them, but yes. It's always interesting when the escorts realize they get paid to do nothing. I've learned to bring cards and board games on those busts. The FBI has a list of escorts who know better than to snitch on undercover agents, and they're compensated well for their discretion. In exchange, we turn a blind eye as long as they keep their activities clean."

"Please explain to me how an escort keeps her activities clean. This seems like important information."

"She's not involved with drug or sex trafficking. We ignore evidence of standard sex work, although most law enforcement does nowadays. It's pointless."

"With people like my mom around, it'd be pretty stupid to prosecute sex workers."

"Gotta keep the lawyers busy," he countered.

I wondered what Kenneth would think when he found out Dad was a defense attorney and had been for thirty years. "Don't like lawyers?"

"I like to consider myself a brave man, but little scares me more than a lawyer on a mission. They don't play fair, jail bird."

"So, if I ever need to put you in your place, I'd just need to find a lawyer?" I laughed. Dad would enjoy having fun with the one who'd arrested me. I could have fun with him, too, especially if I lucked out and snagged mandatory pro bono hours on a case involving Kenneth.

I bet his expression in the courtroom would be priceless.

"You're a wicked, wicked woman, jail bird. Has anyone ever told you that?"

"Ma sometimes does in her saddest, most disappointed voice."

"That comes as no surprise, angel and all. I had no idea your life was so interesting. How'd you end up being a dancer of all things?"

Fortunately for me, I'd worked hard to hide my dirty little lawyer secret and had a canned answer for him. "It's hard to get a job sometimes when you're infected with lycanthropy. Employers don't care if you're not contagious; to them, it's just a matter of time. They're especially hard on unmated lycanthrope women in New York. They expect us to drop everything the instant a man catches our attention. Stupid, if you ask me. Gotta eat."

"They expect your mate to pay for everything. Lycanthropes are shockingly conservative on that issue. I've never met a lycanthrope man who wasn't determined to keep his woman from lifting a finger unless she wanted to. And I've never met a lycanthrope woman who wasn't determined to do as much heavy lifting as possible. I swear, lycanthropes are wired to have daily power plays with each other."

"Now take all that and add a succubus and angel into the mix."

"Have you ever considered getting kidnapped? It might be safer. I might be willing to soil my perfect record and arrange for you to disappear. It'd be cruel to force you to return to that insanity."

I laughed. "No, but I tried running away once. It didn't work out well. If Ma thought she could get away with it, she'd lock me in the basement for life."

"If you don't want to be kidnapped for your own safety, please invite me to a family dinner one day. I'd love to see this chaos for myself."

"I'll think about it as thanks for bailing me out today."

Kenneth's smile promised trouble.

FBI AGENTS MADE a lot more money than I thought. Kenneth's room was a suite on the top floor, one with two bedrooms, a living room that put my parents' to shame, and a bathtub worth committing felonies for. I wished Dad the best of luck defending my case, as I'd have no shame in confessing my crimes along with how I managed to get the damned thing out of the resort when it was large enough to fit two comfortably.

"I'm not sure what you're thinking, but every time I've seen a woman with that expression, it's either led straight to trouble or an arrest."

"There's no middle ground with you, is there? It's like you jump straight to arrest as your solution to life's problems."

"I've found a few problems arrest definitely doesn't solve."

"Oh? Do tell." I set my bags near the door until Kenneth claimed the bedroom he wanted as his, exploring the rest of the suite. There was a second bathroom with the same, glorious tub. I pointed at it, then turned and pointed at the matching one across the room. "What is this insanity?"

"The master bedroom has one, too. I haven't figured out why the entry has a full bath in it, but I'm not going to complain. I might watch television and decide it's too far to walk to the other bathroom to take a hot bath."

"That would be terribly tragic, having to walk an additional five feet to go to your own bathroom."

Kenneth laughed and chucked his bag in the direction of the nearest bedroom. "Honestly, I had no idea I was getting this room. My boss made the reservation, I just paid for it out of my vacation pay. I refused to take off the three weeks he wanted, but I splurged and cashed out two extra weeks of vacation. He allowed it. Probably didn't want to get into an argument with me over it."

"How tragic for you, being subjected to such a nice room for a week."

"It was perfect for rescuing my favorite jail bird from needing a rental from some slum hotel in Boulder."

"When in need of rescue, this jail bird summons either the angel or the lycanthrope."

"Not the succubus?"

"The last time I asked Mom for help, Dad had to bail her out of prison, and Ma couldn't even blame her for it."

"What the hell sort of trouble did you get into?"

I laughed. "I needed one of my parents to talk to my teacher. It didn't end well."

"Dare I ask how old you were?"

"Twelve. My teacher was a woman, and Mom went out of her way to make her uncomfortable. It was in retaliation for calling me a miniature slut because of my pedigree. Mom was arrested for disrupting the peace and trespassing, but the charges were dismissed when the police verified she was really my mother and attending a parent-teacher meeting."

"Your teacher called the child of an angel a miniature slut?"

I held up my hands in surrender. "Don't ask me. I think it was Ma's turn to get left off my papers. Most forms don't have a third spot for my second mother, so they fight over who gets to be listed."

"Sounds tough."

"Only when my teacher wants a parent-teacher meeting and Mom's the one who gets to handle it. Ma? Ma's great; no one doubts the word of an angel, especially one indignant at the very idea I might have flaws in my schoolwork."

"Did you have flaws in your schoolwork?"

"I was top of the class from the day I stepped into school until the day I graduated, because nothing is worse than angelic disappointment. I didn't even dare to get detention. Mom was so disappointed I didn't skip school even once."

Kenneth shook his head, his brightest smile making an appearance. "This explains so much. Your mother, the succubus, took you to a bar, got you drunk, and had you snort pixie dust so you wouldn't be a sheltered little flower for the rest of your life, and I was the lucky bastard who got to handle your arrest."

"Lucky?" I dragged my bags to the second bedroom, wondering how things could've gone so wrong that I was in Kenneth's suite for an entire week. The flight had tested the limits of my dignity and patience. If I didn't watch out, I might end up liking the man, something I'd never live down. Under no circumstances was I supposed to like the FBI agent who'd cuffed me, shoved me into his car, and gotten the order for me to stay overnight in solitary confinement thanks to my mother's mission to teach me about life as an adult. "You have got to be kidding me."

"I consider myself very lucky. That double booking was pretty rotten, though. Think about it this way. You got an upgrade."

"I'm afraid to ask how much this upgrade is going to cost me. I'd gotten an early booking discount on my room."

"Please don't worry about it. I'm paying for the room as it is, and it's not like adding you to my reservation adds to the price. If it makes you feel better, just give me what you would've paid when we get back to New York. Relax."

Arguing with him would stress us both out, so I nodded. I dug into my bag and fetched my bikini, already regretting I'd followed Mom's advice on swimwear, which meant Kenneth Bernard would get a close look at a lot of skin. The dinky scraps of material Mom insisted on barely toed the line of modesty. Why had I inherited my sense of right or wrong from Ma's contribution of genes? "I came the night before specifically so I could go swimming in the pool before the retreat. Would you like to join me?"

"After how much I paid for this week, you better believe I'm going to join you. My daddy taught me the first rule of travel: leave no amenity unturned."

"Your daddy has a firm grasp of common sense." I discovered the bathroom attached to my bedroom, skipped inside, and locked the door behind me. He'd get a good look at everything else, but I'd leave a few secrets for the man I tagged, bagged, married, and infected with my virus, cursing him to a lifetime of bird-brained jokes and more feathers than anyone ever needed.

I think it's important to state I didn't do it.

FOR A FULLY BOOKED HOTEL, few people were out and about, and as far as I could tell, we had the indoor pool to ourselves. I liked the open space encased in windows, which let the sunlight in and kept the weather out.

I would've liked the pool a lot more if there hadn't been a body floating in the middle. Given the amount of time we'd spent walking around the glass-enclosed space without having seen anyone inside, I had no doubt she was dead beyond resuscitation.

Then I remembered it took time for a body to float, and she lacked any of the signs of having been dead for too long. All of my education pointed to one unpleasant fact: she'd been dead before she'd entered the water, preserving the air in her lungs, keeping her body afloat.

I sucked in a deep breath and glanced at Kenneth, who had decided to bring his phone for some unfathomable reason. "Kenneth?"

He halted, his eyes locked on the screen. "What's up, jail bird?"

"First, I think it's important to state I didn't do it."

He jerked his head up and stared at me. "Pardon?"

I pointed at the woman's body. While I'd specialized in prosecuting homicides, I hadn't expected to be someone to discover a body. At a loss of what to say or do, I shrugged.

Kenneth frowned, looked at where I pointed, and spat curses. "Jesus Christ."

"Logically, I know this isn't the case, but my first thought? I thought bodies were supposed to sink after drowning. But then I remembered that bodies float after a while." I'd let the FBI agent figure out she'd likely been killed before being tossed into the pool.

"I don't think she's been dead long enough to float. There's no other signs of decomposition. That means she was probably dumped into the pool after death." Kenneth redirected his attention to his phone, dialed a number, and held it to his ear. "Hello. My name's Kenneth Bernard, FBI, and I'm at Mountain Gully Resort outside of Boulder. There's a deceased Caucasian female in the indoor pool. Yes, I'll hold."

Kenneth scowled, tapping his foot on the tiles while he waited. "Yes, ma'am. She's floating face down, unmoving, and there are no signs of life. Had there been, I would've jumped in to help her, obviously."

I shook my head at the implication either one of us would let a woman drown. I gave it an hour before I had to make an unpleasant phone call to Ma so we could verify our alibi in an unassailable fashion.

Sometimes, having an angel for a mother was a pain in

my ass, but it paid off in spades when I was innocent of wrongdoing.

"Yes, ma'am. We'll be here waiting. I'm accompanied by a friend. She was the one who discovered the body. We'd come down to the pool from our room for a swim. Yes, I'll hold."

At the rate Kenneth was tapping his foot, he'd punch a hole through the floor. We hadn't even had a chance to take our shoes off.

"No, ma'am. I have no idea who the woman is. She's face down in the pool. Yes, I'll hold."

"She likes putting you on hold, doesn't she?"

"She's dispatching officers and an ambulance to our location. Normally, she'd keep talking on the line, but this is my work phone, so she's able to confirm I'm in law enforcement. Well, I hope she confirmed it, otherwise she's going to have a bad time when her supervisor reviews her calls."

I stared at the body. "Why would someone dump a body in a pool she wouldn't normally be able to drown in? Under any normal circumstance, she'd just stand up and be fine. That water's not deep."

"Don't know. That's a very good question. That's also why I didn't go in to pull her out. The police will want to have a look over the whole scene when they arrive. I'm sorry, but we'll be questioned. That's probably not how you wanted today to go."

"Truer words were never spoken. I'm not going to be arrested, am I?" I knew we wouldn't be arrested, but I wanted to see what he'd say.

"If we're really unlucky, we'll be asked to go to the station for questioning." His brow furrowed, and he held up a finger. "Yes, ma'am. That's correct. We'll be here. Thank you."

He hung up, shaking his head.

"That doesn't look promising."

"There's an unfortunate statistic where the person who calls in about a death is the cause of death. Her tone implied she thought this was the case. Drownings are difficult, as there's often a loss of evidence."

I loved my ma, and I'd make sure she knew it within the next five minutes. "Can I borrow your phone? I'll cover the not guilty of drowning someone part of things. I hope you don't have an aversion to angels."

He offered me his phone. "Not at all. I've worked with them many a time. It's the archangels who put me on edge."

Archangels put me on edge, too, and I'd met more than my fair share of them. "Israfil's terrifying."

"Which one's that?"

Crap. I'd used the Arabic version of the archangel's name again. If Ma found out, she'd scold me. Again. "Sorry, Raphael."

"Which one's that?"

"He's one of the archangels who can trumpet in the end of everything. Michael's the other one. It's a bit muddled, honestly. They might be the same archangel for all I know. Point stands, though. He's terrifying."

"That's a good reason to be terrified of him."

"I certainly thought so. I think I hurt his feelings when he visited Ma. I ran away. I may have screamed. It's not my fault. I was little, and Ma kept telling me stories about him!"

"Being honest with you, I've never known whether to think of an angel as a male or female."

"You think of them in whatever gender they currently are because only an idiot judges an angel about their current gender of choice. When I met Raphael, he was male."

"How could you even tell?"

"His voice. They change their voice to match their currently chosen gender. So, Ma sounds like a woman right now. After Dad dies, who knows? She'll probably return to the heavens for a while to mourn. That's typical."

"Fortunately for your Ma, lycanthropes live a long time."

"That's not a boon in Mom's book, because she's stuck with Dad, too. Ma and Dad won't let her escape. It's fun watching her try, though."

"Anything else I should know?"

"If you don't want Ma knowing something, don't even think it. Also, don't lie. Don't even think a lie. Ma hates liars. I lied to her once. She spanked my ass so hard I couldn't sit for three days. You won't ever catch another lie coming out of this mouth ever again, not when Ma might hear me, no, sir."

Kenneth put his phone in my hand. "Just call before you get so nervous you can't hold the phone."

"What makes you think I'm nervous?"

"You're babbling worse than a brook, jail bird."

Damn it. I firmed my grip on Kenneth's phone and dialed Mom's number as I still couldn't accept Ma conjuring a phone at her whim.

"Baby girl, why are you calling me already? Also, you left the chain on the lawn. You're supposed to use the chain to catch yourself a man. Have you had any luck catching yourself a man? You need to get laid."

"Mom!" I wailed. "That's not funny. And you knew I was going on a plane. I can't take a chain on the plane for man-catching purposes. Will you be serious? I need you to put Ma on the phone."

"Why didn't you call her phone?"

"I hate when she does that hand waving summon her phone thing. It creeps me out."

"Baby, you're an idiot. How would you even know? She would've done it before she answered."

Mom had a point, which supported Kenneth's belief I was nervous. I preferred thinking of myself as appropriately rattled. "There's a woman's body in the swimming pool at the resort, and a friend and I found her. The cops will think we did it, and I don't want to be arrested for something I didn't even do." A whine slipped out, and I grimaced.

"That's different. Your trip's going to the birds real quick, isn't it?"

"Just a bit. Before I found the body, it'd only been a disaster. Now it's an unmitigated disaster."

"Well, hold onto your panties. I'll go get your ma."

"Thanks."

It didn't take long for Ma to come on the line. "Your mom says you found a body, Emma?"

I wondered what it said about my life that an angel calling me by my name counted as some much needed normality. "Yeah. She's floating in the pool. I wanted to know if you'd come to the resort and convince the police officers I didn't kill her." A soft pop announced Ma's arrival, and I hung up, offering the phone back to Kenneth. One day, I'd ask how she figured out how to teleport to a place she'd never been before. "Thanks, Ma."

"It appears I should've brought the chain with me," Ma replied. She held out her hand and Mom's phone popped out of existence. "I really need to stop taking Louisa's phone with me when I go. It's such a bad habit. Remind me to get her a bottle of wine on the way home. That should keep her quiet for five minutes."

"No chains," I begged. "Please. I've had a bad enough day."

"Beyond the body, what's wrong? And yes, there's no way you were responsible for the body. She's been there for at least an hour. I peeked. The mortals will have to do the rest of the investigating work on their own."

"They double booked my room."

"That's annoying."

"And the hotel is full."

"That's even more annoying. What are you doing now?" Ma asked, and the amusement in her tone implied she'd done more than peek at the woman's body in the past.

"Agent Bernard offered a room in his suite for the retreat so I wouldn't have to drive to some slum hotel in Boulder every day."

"You're the sex on a stick who arrested her when Louisa nipped the high-grade pixie dust and convinced Emma here to snort it like a hooligan?"

I groaned, bowed my head, and wished I'd inherited Ma's ability to disappear. What had I done to deserve Ma at her worst?

"Yes, ma'am. I am."

I couldn't tell which part he was confirming. Did he view himself as sex on a stick? I couldn't say he was wrong, but if he did, I'd have to pop his ego bubble a little. "Please, Ma," I begged.

"He's single, in case you were wondering. He's also clean of any of those annoying illnesses humans get. Don't forget to show him your cute little card if you decide you're ready to settle down. He has a stable job, he's up for a promotion soon, and he's in a good position to take care of a cranky, pregnant lycanthrope."

Was avoiding arrest worth the price I'd pay avoiding arrest? My face burned. "Ma!"

"Emma, you're not a little girl anymore. I'm going to have to have a talk with Louisa, or we're never going to be able to get rid of you. Fly from the roost, you ground-bound chick."

"Chick?" I worried about the curiosity in Kenneth's tone.

"Chick. That's what you call a baby swan, and that's what my little girl here is. She's still in her baby down. I'm sure she'll get around to feathering out and leave the nest one of these days."

Kenneth's brows rose. "You're not a wolf?"

"Ma, please," I whispered.

"The boy needs to know what he's getting into. Trust me. Logically, I'd known your father was a swan, but I hadn't anticipated how troublesome swans are. He has an entire flock of baby chickens right now because we are not adding another swan to the mix until our first one fledges. You can handle a swan, Kenneth. Take her. Please. I'll pay you handsomely."

"This must be the dowry offer I've read about in history books."

Did the woman in the pool want company? What was an extra body? It wouldn't take long for me to drown, but I'd sink rather than float. Maybe they'd leave me long enough to float, too?

Ma placed her hand on my head. "No."

"Was that a no to the dowry?"

"Oh, I'm sorry. No, it wasn't. Emma was thinking childish thoughts again, so I thought I'd nip that in the bud. A dowry would be arranged upon your acceptance of our daughter, I assure you. We'd modernize it, as a herd of goats or horses wouldn't be particularly useful to a modern man like yourself, but it'll be appropriate for a young couple starting a family."

"Selling your child is illegal, Ma."

"I'm not selling you. I'm merely greasing the wheels so this strapping man won't resist quite as much when you give him your card. Consider it a compensation package for the week or two of effort he'll have to put in to secure his status and earn your dowry."

Why, why, why couldn't I kill angels? "Ma!"

"You wouldn't kill your ma, Emma. Why are you so embarrassed? Where did we go wrong with you?"

"Why do you think you went wrong with me? That's not even fair."

"Most women lose their virginity by twenty-one. You're a bit behind the curve. You could test the waters for the entire week and be able to change your mind unless your virus finally gets around to maturing. You're behind the curve there, too."

Kenneth's mouth dropped open, but before he had a chance to say anything, the door behind us banged open and several police officers hurried inside with several hotel staff in tow. "We got a call there was a body?" the older man leading the line asked.

He reminded me of a much older version of Dad, already tired of the shit he had to deal with after being at work for an hour.

We pointed at the pool.

"Officer, I'd like to simplify matters for you some and verify the alibis of these two, as they found the body and the police have an unfortunate tendency to automatically blame the discoverers for the crime. While that does happen, this is not the case. Children, do tell them where you were."

"Well, four and a half hours ago, approximately, we were in New York waiting for our flight to come here," I said, grateful the conversation about my shortcomings and lack of a relationship with Kenneth would be delayed. "After we arrived at the airport, we checked in. My room was double booked, so Kenneth offered me the second bedroom in his suite, which I accepted. We're both here to attend a retreat this week. Anyway, we went upstairs, agreed we wanted to go swimming, and came down to the pool. I spotted her after we came inside. That's when Kenneth called."

"She's telling the truth," Ma confirmed.

"And neither of you know this woman?" the cop asked. "You touched nothing?"

"We walked in and stopped after I spotted her. I don't know if I know her. We can't see her face, sir."

"She's telling the truth."

"It's the same on my end of things. I don't know if I know her, as I can't see her face. I'm in the FBI, but my badge is upstairs if you need it for your records."

The cops focused on Kenneth, looking him over.

"Yeah, it surprised me, too," I muttered.

Kenneth shot a glare at me.

"What? You don't look like a cop, an FBI agent, or anything like that. I could buy firefighter with a little convincing." I shrugged and held my hands up in surrender. "Just telling the truth here."

"That she is. Try to be a little more polite, Emma."

"You're the one trying to marry me off to him. I don't have to be polite."

"It would be nice if you were polite for the moment. You may indulge in your typical rebellion after we speak to the nice police officers."

The cops returned to scrutinizing me. "Do you know each other, miss?"

I sighed. "She's one of my mothers."

"That's convenient for you."

I yanked my hair. "What the bloody hell is convenient about having an angel for a mother? Are you mad? I bet you could lie to your parents. Oh, no. Not in my house, sir. Never in—"

Kenneth placed his hand over my mouth. "I'm sorry. She's had a very stressful day, and I doubt she's seen a body before."

Ma chuckled, and as always, her laughter soothed. "I'd be offended, but it's true. She gets away with exactly nothing in our household. If you'd like a double verification, I can send for another angel, but I'd like to remind you I am an angel, and angels cannot lie."

The cop waved his hand. "This simplifies things for us. We'll need your contact information for additional questioning, but if an angel is confirming you know nothing, you know nothing."

"We know nothing. I suppose we might if we recognize the victim," Kenneth replied.

"Take pictures and get her out," the cop ordered. "Get forensics here sometime today!"

One of the cops stripped off all his electronics, ditched his pants and vest, and jumped into the water, wading to the woman and pulling her towards the edge. The other two helped grab her under the arms and pull her onto the tiles.

Relief surged through me.

I didn't know her.

"Never seen her in my life," Kenneth reported.

"I've never seen her before, either."

"Both speak the truth," Ma confirmed.

"All right. Give me your contact information, and if we have any other questions, we'll give you a call."

We gave him our phone numbers, addresses, and itinerary for the next week before he gave us permission to leave. I almost made it to the doors before Ma caught up, linked her arm with mine, and prevented my escape. "Where do you think you're going, little chick?"

"I'm going to bed so I can hide under the covers for the rest of my life."

Ma sighed. "You were trouble from the day you were born."

"Would you like to see our room, ma'am?" Kenneth said, holding the door open so we could escape the pool and the police working to solve the mystery of the woman's death.

"I'd love to. Thank you. See, Emma? That wasn't hard, was it?"

No matter what I said, I lost somehow. "He's politer than I am. I'm sorry."

"You've had a hard day," Ma murmured, releasing my arm to rub my back. "After I see you to your room, I'll head home and tell the others what happened."

I assumed she'd tell them in the worst way possible, ensuring they'd come to Boulder themselves for the duration of my retreat. Accepting inevitable defeat, I sighed and said, "Thank you."

"We're not that bad, you know."

I wished my ma had a head so I could look her in the eyes. "Yes, you are."

"So cruel. And to think I helped bring you into the world. Don't you love your ma?"

"On Mondays, Wednesdays, and Fridays. Mom gets Tuesdays, Thursdays, and Saturdays, and I hate you both equally on Sundays."

"You cheeky little liar."

Kenneth elbowed me. "I thought you said angels hated when people lie to them."

"I'm telling her I love her in an unconventional manner. That's all right. Angels understand sarcasm. Usually."

"I see the rules are not as simple as I believed."

"The rules are never simple when angels are involved."

"That's the honest truth. It's no fun if you warn him about everything."

"He saved me from having to call you to pay for a rental and a hotel room for a week. He's getting every single warning I can think of, so when I have to pay up and intro- duce him to Mom and Dad, he survives."

"You're introducing him properly?"

"He seems interested in seeing just how chaotic our house can be around dinner time. Since he spared me from checking into a different hotel and having to beg you for money, I'm going to humor him."

Ma reached over and patted Kenneth's head. "I wish you the best of luck. You're going to need it. Please give some thought about anything you'd like in the dowry. I suspect you'll earn every gift we offer you for dealing with her. She's a chip off her father's block."

Instead of visiting our room as she'd threatened, Ma disappeared. I narrowed my eyes, as she hadn't vanished with her customary flash of light. "Ma, I know you're still there. Stop being an asshole."

Ma huffed, and moved to stand behind me. "I was only going to sneak into your room and check his intentions. That's important."

"Or you could just ask him what his intentions are and spare me from your lunacy."

"Fine. What are your intentions, you?"

"Ma!"

"What?"

"He has a name."

"I know."

"You should use his name."

"I don't want to."

Why did Ma always have to test my patience? "You don't have to answer her, Kenneth."

"I intend on figuring out something for dinner and discovering how nice a jet tub feels after a rather soured afternoon. I may or may not order a bottle or two of wine and indulge before I bloody my feet tomorrow in what will likely be a very damaging day for my pride and ego."

"And your intentions with my daughter?"

"You're the one who wants to pay me to take her off your hands. Why are you asking me this?"

"Ugh. He's just as bad as your father." Ma vanished in a flash of silver, which meant only one thing: she'd returned to the heavens to stir trouble because she could.

"You have a very strange family, jail bird. I think you need some wine even more than I do. Shall we?"

"Why the hell not?"

FIVE

Sure, jail bird. Whatever you say.

As we'd both gotten ready to swim, we decided to share the communal tub along with a bottle of red wine. Kenneth brought the room service menu, and we dedicated most of our attention to the serious problem of dinner rather than focus on the reason we weren't swimming and unwinding before the retreat officially began.

"Did you know they're doing a full-week partner assignment?" Kenneth asked, setting aside the leather-bound menu in favor of his wine. "There's going to be pissy partners."

I laughed, grabbed my wine glass, and saluted him with it. "Best news I've heard today. I don't care; I don't usually have a partner, so I'm used to working with anyone I'm assigned. Some really don't work well with new people, and it's hilarious watching them meltdown because they aren't sure how to work with someone else. It'll make them better dancers if they can get over themselves."

"It's more unusual you don't have a partner. Don't you work for the same theatre all the time?"

"I'm a floater. I fill in for any woman on any team, so I have to know all the routines for all the active performances in case someone is sick or injured. I'm paid to show up, learn the routines, and perform if necessary."

"Wouldn't you make more if you weren't a floater?"

I shrugged. "Sure, I suppose. The theater came up with the idea after they had to cancel a show because of a missing dancer. So, they hired a few versatile dancers who could learn a routine quickly. I'm one of them. I work full time and coordinate with all the troupes who perform at the theater, making sure we have enough backup dancers ready if they need us."

"You do management work along with dancing?"

"I'd consider it more coordination than management. It keeps me busy when I'm not in the lineup to dance. I also help backstage if I'm not performing."

"I guess it's hard having the virus without it being mature, isn't it? A lot of companies refuse to employ lycanthropes. I expect the laws will change eventually to prevent discrimination, but it'll be hard in certain fields."

I snorted. "I can understand why. Putting lycanthropes in fields where they can be easily provoked could shoot the infection rate up. Some fields just aren't good for lycanthropes. What pisses me off is we're considered dumber than the uninfected. Being able to shift into an animal doesn't mean we're animals in the intellect department."

"There are plenty of smart lycanthropes within the FBI. Most of the ones who go out into the field have the hybrid form, however."

"I never understood that. Why would you put the lycanthropes most likely to be able to infect someone closest to the public? The hybrid form doesn't grant better control."

"Does your father have the hybrid form?"

I took another drink of my wine and wondered how to answer him. The truth made me look like a bad daughter, but it was the only answer I could realistically give him. "I don't know. I haven't asked. My virus isn't mature enough for me to shift, so it hasn't been a priority for me. If I ever shift, I'll worry about if I'll have the hybrid form then."

"That makes sense. As it seems I've found uncomfortable territory, would you prefer room service tonight or would you like to go out for dinner? There are a few good restaurants within a few miles from here, and the resort has a restaurant."

"Let's try the restaurant. I don't get to go out too often, and once the retreat starts, we're going to be subjected to whatever they think is healthy for us," I replied, swirling my wine in the glass before taking another sip. "If we go to the restaurant, we can spread out the wine. Nothing sucks more than trying to dance with a hangover."

"I haven't tried to dance with a hangover before, so I'm going to take your word for it. I expect by the time this week is over, the partner I'm assigned to will want to kill me. I can dance, but I can't dance to the level of a professional. The retreat needed an extra man, and I barely met the minimum requirements. Should I bring flowers as an apology in advance?"

I laughed and waved him off. "Do your best. If you get a diva, there's not much you can do about it. This isn't a competition, so it's not like you're going to hurt her chances for the future. It's for expansion of skills. Worry more about having a good time and don't worry too much about your partner."

"Why do I have a feeling most other dancers aren't going to have the same mentality?"

"I'd say you're smart, but you mouthed off to an angel. She's probably visiting the heavens now waiting to smite you for your mouthy ways."

Kenneth laughed. "The funny thing about this? I wasn't even trying to mouth off that time."

"You're going to have to work on that. When stuck with an angel, a succubus, and a lycanthrope, your ability to mouth off might be the only thing capable of saving you from a triple dose of snark coupled with parental disappointment."

"Maybe I should have insisted you visit my parents instead. They just have a disgusting magic rating and inflated egos. They also work in law enforcement. It's a family tradition."

I snorted. "Sounds safer to me. Despite appearances, I can go out without doing anything illegal. It was just the one time!"

"Sure, jail bird. Whatever you say."

Wine and a big dinner conspired to create an early bedtime, and I only made it to the couch before I crashed and burned. Kenneth laughed, and the sound was so pleasant I fought sleep to listen. The next thing I knew, my phone blared to warn me I needed to get my ass out of bed. I reached for it, fell off the couch, and smacked into the carpet. A thick, warm blanket fell onto me, and I questioned if I wanted to get up to turn the alarm off.

I groaned, reached for the insufferable device my parents

insisted I carry with me at all times, and fumbled for the button to silence it.

"You make the cutest little honk when you snore. I assume this is something you inherited from your father."

Fuck. Kenneth.

For ten whole seconds, I'd forgotten I shared a hotel room with him. Stupid wine. Stupid, ridiculously expensive dinner at a ridiculously fancy resort hotel restaurant. My contribution to the groceries would be every package of ramen I could get my hands on for a month making up for my indulgence, snuck in whenever my parents weren't looking so they wouldn't go on another tirade over my poor life choices.

At least Kenneth had the decency to give me something worth feigning indignant rage over. "I do not honk."

"You honk. I even recorded it as irrefutable evidence of your rather unique snore. In good news, you don't honk loudly. In even better news, I got all my laughing out of the way while you were sleeping. I'll even be a generous soul and promise I won't betray your honking secret. I'm so generous I won't even blackmail you over it."

While breaking my phone would summon the wrath of all three of my parents, breaking it over Kenneth's egotistical head would be worth it. Instead of assaulting him for daring to tease me about my snore, I crawled from beneath the blanket and headed for the safety of my bedroom. "How long do we have until breakfast?"

"I'd love to be your social secretary for the week. We have an hour to head down for breakfast, then we have an hour-long lecture about what to expect for the rest of the week, which will include our partner assignments. After that, hell begins."

"Why did you even pick this if you think it's hell?"

"My other choices were to work at a cattle ranch for a week or go sailing. While I don't mind the water, fishing for a week without returning to land even once does not seem like my idea of a good time. As I've never ridden a horse before, I figured the cattle ranch was a disaster waiting to happen. I can dance, just not at your level."

"I don't doubt it. You'll be fine. I need to take a shower and get changed. I'll be ready in ten."

"What's this? You're one of the mythical women who doesn't take an eternity in the bathroom in the morning? Obviously, I should've recommended house arrest. In my house. I'm assuming, judging from your ma's insistence on offering a dowry, you're single?"

"Obviously. The only boys I've considered are lycanthropes, and none of them met my father's approval, so in classical lycanthrope father fashion, he drove them off. I think Mom took me to that bar to find me someone, gave up hope, and hooked me up with pixie dust to take off the edge of eternal disappointment in the bachelor pool." I shrugged, grabbed the bag with my dance apparel, and hauled it into my bathroom. "How are you even single?"

"I've been told I'm married to my job. Should I take that question as an expression of interest?"

Ma would need to suffer the pains of hell for putting me in this situation. Or, more accurately, for worsening the situation. "Take it however you want. I need a shower before I can deal with this."

He'd find out soon enough my family was the number one reason I'd probably die an old, wrinkled, virgin.

I BLITZED through my morning shower and dressed in a dance leotard. Not certain I'd need it, I brought my bag with my variety of tulle skirts and my tutu so I'd be prepared. So I wouldn't come across as promiscuous, I wore my classic black leotard with matching tulle to offer the illusion I wasn't wearing a skin-tight outfit leaving little to the imagination.

Some days, I felt more covered when I wore my bikini. Armed with all the apparel I thought I'd need, I emerged from the bathroom.

Kenneth went the saner route, wearing a pair of light sweats which would work with almost any style of dancing. Had I been a little wiser and less of a skinflint, I would've invested in a pair of leggings and a tight top or new leotard for the venture.

Lesson learned. Next time, I'd budget for a shopping trip of more comfortable clothing for a dance retreat. That way, when everything went wrong, I'd look good, be a step ahead of everyone else, and stay cozy while dancing.

"I'm going for being the most casually dressed at the retreat. None of the ladies will feel bad when they see me dressed like I couldn't give a damn."

"Do you give a damn?"

"Not in the slightest. It's nice to get away from wearing a suit for a change. I wear jeans at home, though. But jeans don't offer enough mobility for a lot of dance styles, or so I've been led to believe."

"You're fine."

"Do you really need to take an entire bag with you? I'm not sure you'll need whatever you've got in it."

I stared at the bag, stared at him, and scowled as the realization sank in he was probably right. "But what if I need a tutu instead of a tulle?"

"You can come back to the room and fetch the tutu? I bet you could slip the room key and your bank card in your leotard somewhere."

I could, so I retrieved the two cards from my bag, slipped them into one of my card sleeves I kept around for the purposes of using my breasts for storage, and stuffed them into my cleavage.

"Not quite what I had in mind, but I should've known better."

"When nature provides you with a treasury, you use it. Where else would I put it?"

Kenneth pointed at my side.

"I'd get jabbed with the cards when I had to move. I still might get jabbed, but at least they're easy to access. Were I a less moral individual, I could smuggle all sorts of things in my cleavage and no one would ever know."

"It's not even eight, and I've already learned so many new things today."

"I can think of one thing you've learned today."

"You honk in your sleep, you bounce awake when your phone goes off, which resulted in you hitting the floor, you take showers faster than I do, and you store things in your cleavage."

It was going to be a long week, and at a loss of what else to do, I flipped him the bird and headed for the door. "I do not honk!"

Kenneth laughed.

I COLLIDED with my father leaving the elevator, and he caught me in a headlock before I could bolt for safety. I squawked, struggling to keep my balance when he changed directions and headed for the lobby. In typical Dad fashion, he didn't say a word; he'd wait until we were somewhere more private to tear into me.

"I didn't do anything this time, you bird brain." I struggled in his grip, digging my fingers into his forearm. "Come on, give me a break here. I'm going to be late for breakfast. I can't dance on an empty stomach."

"Mr. Sansaul?" Kenneth blurted.

Dad halted, twisting around. "You're the one she's sleeping with?"

What the hell had Ma told Mom and Dad? "He offered to share his two-bedroom suite because the hotel was overbooked, Dad. I didn't sleep with him."

"She slept on the couch because she forgot she needed to walk the extra fifteen feet to reach her bed, actually. But close enough. That couch isn't big enough for two. Anyway, an angel promised me a dowry if I took her. The honking in her sleep is a concern, but otherwise, she doesn't seem to have any bad habits."

"Please don't listen to a word he says, Dad. Please," I begged.

"You were offered a dowry?"

"I was informed I needed to come up with a list of things roughly equivalent to a herd of animals. I haven't quite figured out how much a herd of animals is worth, yet."

Dad sighed and loosened his hold. "Emma, why are you staying in Agent Bernard's room?"

"The hotel double booked my room. He felt sorry for me."

Kenneth chuckled. "It seemed a pity to make her hike

twenty minutes to the nearest hotel for a week. My suite has two bedrooms; it made sense to offer her the second bedroom."

"I came to Colorado why?" Dad grunted, turned, and bellowed, "Louisa, you shameless hussy!"

I covered my face with my hands. "Mom's not a hussy, Dad. She's just cranky she's sorta monogamous."

Mom made her appearance, and to my relief, she was in her human form, dressed in a blazer and a skirt that showed off her assets for my father's enjoyment. "Oh, stop your whining, baby. You were bored and coming to Colorado seemed like fun at the time. The damned girl hasn't jumped him yet, so don't get your panties in a bunch."

"Louisa. Was there something you forgot to tell me?"

"Not that I can think of."

"You heard nothing about a certain angel offering a dowry for Emma?"

"Oh. That. I figured it's her money, so she can do whatever she wants with it. I might play nice this time and match it. She wants another baby, George. Are you really going to come between an angel and her next child? Honestly, I'm looking forward to it. We don't get a new chick unless we get rid of this one. Be grateful he's gotten the approval of both mothers. Behave for once in your life."

I bowed my head and sighed. "You wanted to meet them, Kenneth. This is your fault. Ma must have heard you thinking about it, so here we are. I hope you're happy with yourself."

"I had no idea your father was a defense attorney. I also had no idea he was a defense attorney with a hobby of annoying the FBI over drug use cases. This only makes this so much more amusing, jail bird."

"You were the arresting officer?" Dad sucked in a breath and hissed, a precursor for him losing his temper and sprouting feathers.

"It was one of the best arrests of my life. There I am, kicking back and relaxing, when this succubus cons a young lady into snorting pixie dust. It would've been fine if she hadn't taken the highest-grade stuff in production. It took three rounds of neutralizer to fix that mess, and she had to be kept in solitary." Kenneth snickered and shook his head. "She just loves it when I call her jail bird."

Why were men assholes? "Please go home, Dad. Everything is just fine."

"But I don't want to go home. I managed to get a room here due to a cancellation. Your mothers talked me into this trip and promised I'd be able to get to the bottom of this nonsense. I was not told you were sleeping with an FBI agent, the one who'd arrested you for illegal pixie dust usage."

"I'm not sleeping with him, Dad," I whispered.

"Well, why not?"

My life had turned upside down on me. "What happened to you attempting to murder every single man who looked at me twice?"

"They weren't FBI agents with a good record and decent prospects. I wouldn't complain if any of those lycanthropes who'd come sniffing around were cops with the hybrid form. By the time he's contagious, he'll be ready to retire from street work."

"Are you planning my career for me, Mr. Sansaul?" Kenneth's mouth dropped open, and I huffed my triumph that he'd been sideswiped by my father. Most days, I felt like he looked, stunned my parents could be so damned strange.

"I'm just giving you the facts, boy. You're gonna be a long time maturing her virus. She's been trying to mature hers since she was just a little chick. It hasn't gotten her anywhere. Maybe you'll have better luck. Once you're infected, she'll be determined to protect her turf. Our lot's pretty territorial."

"I had no idea swans were territorial."

"Aggressive, too. Check online if you want an idea of what you're getting into, except I'm much, much larger than a natural swan."

"How much larger?"

"Well, the last time I got into a fight with a wolf, he spent three days out for the count and needed transfusions from his pack."

I sighed. "He likes hospitalizing lycanthropes who come calling. He tells them to fight him, he hospitalizes them, and they never come back."

"I'm starting to understand why things are as they are. Not to cut this short, Mr. Sansaul, but if we don't get breakfast, we're going to be stuck with some high-intensity workouts on empty stomachs. We might snap our ankles due to malnutrition."

"I'll find you later," my father swore, giving me a hefty dose of stink eye before stepping away. "You keep an eye on my little girl, Agent Bernard."

"Yes, sir," Kenneth wisely replied.

I pitied him if I did as much as stub a toe. One of my parents would end Kenneth's existence, and I wasn't sure which one.

I FELL on my food like a starved beast. My father held full responsibility for my ravenous appetite, which cost me a small fortune every payday to keep from quivering from hunger and exhaustion. I blamed Mom for my love of good food. I pinned blame on Ma for the slow development of my virus, as my angelic genes likely made it harder for the infection to develop.

While I did substantial damage to the hotel's food supply, Kenneth watched me, his brows rising with every plate of food I packed away. "Had I not witnessed you eating dinner last night, I'd be convinced you haven't eaten in a month. Your food isn't going to escape." He checked the wall clock. "We have plenty of time. Yesterday, I hated the idea of an hour of lectures and inspirational speeches to encourage us to dance, but you're going to need that time to digest, or else you'll be waddling."

"It's Dad's fault. If I don't eat enough for three, I get hungry again in an hour."

"I'm going to have to adjust the dowry requirements to account for feeding you. That's how this works, right? They're paying me off to take care of you for the rest of your life, right?" He smirked, picked up a piece of toast, and pointed it at me. "I'm onto them. They're just tired of feeding two lycanthropes. A second child is just bribery to convince your father to let you out of the nest."

I eyed his toast, leaned forward, and chomped onto it, pulling it out of his hand. To demonstrate I had plenty of room left in the cavernous depths of my stomach, I devoured the piece and attacked one of the bananas I'd grabbed to balance a stack of pancakes, three waffles, a leaning tower of bacon, and the lake of maple syrup I'd need to get me through to lunch. "I don't know what you're talking about."

"You're eating enough for at least five people, jail bird. I'm never looking at 'eat like a bird' the same way ever again, because you're a living vacuum cleaner. If you suck up that food any faster, you'll choke. If you choke, I'll be beaten by an infuriated lycanthrope. Please don't choke."

"You had no idea my father's a lycanthrope, did you?"

"Infection status isn't advertised in courtrooms unless the judge orders it. Law is considered a non-threatening career choice for a lycanthrope. Their clients would know, but few others would unless a request was put in. I don't request infection disclosure, as it has no bearing on cases I'm involved with. Typically, I'm only called in to testify about the arrest, evidence gathered, and my interactions with the defendant."

"Do you face off against my father often?"

"It's going to make work interesting in the future. If I'm saddled with a certain jail bird, I'll have to disclose it every time he's on the defense. And because your father is who he is, he'll enjoy crushing me in court every chance he gets."

I laughed and snagged a piece of bacon, making short work of it. "That's definitely something Dad would do. Dad, grudgingly, said he'd be my lawyer if needed. Very grudgingly. He thought I should represent myself as I'd let Mom get me into trouble."

"That's a bit harsh."

"I recommend you run at the first opportunity."

"And miss the entertainment? I think not. What other surprises are you hiding up your sleeve? Have you considered joining a food-eating competition?"

"Lycanthropes are barred; we have an unfair advantage. I'd get my ass kicked in a lycanthrope-on-lycanthrope competition, though. I've thought about it. Do yourself a favor. Do not look into who won the last competition. It's horrific."

"Good to know. What else should I be on the watch for?"

"I should be asking that of you. I'm pretty sure Ma was joking. She wouldn't actually sell me."

"I think she was assuming you'd go along with the idea without her actually selling you. I was being bribed to accept your advances."

I'd need a lot more bacon to deal with this conversation, but I needed to also conquer my pancakes and waffles before I raised pork prices in Colorado. "What advances?"

"This is going to be more difficult than your parents anticipated, I expect. In our case, I'm sure you could accomplish your goals with strategic use of your bikini and strolling around the suite."

I snorted. "That doesn't sound very difficult."

"I understand when there are battles I won't win. In case you weren't aware, you looked lovely in your bikini."

"Mom suggested it."

"She gave you impeccable advice. She also gave you very skimpy advice."

"There really isn't much to that bikini. My leotards aren't much better."

"I've definitely noticed your leotard fits you very well. I'm concerned. Your father expects me to protect you from unwanted attention."

"I'm sure he was yanking your chain, Kenneth. I'm not completely helpless."

"Only when hopped up on pixie dust?"

"I'm never going to live that down, am I?"

"Not a chance, jail bird."

"I'm not completely helpless. I just have three overprotective parents. The last time I tried to take self-defense courses, I came home covered in bruises. Dad flipped."

"That tells me you're helpless, jail bird. In other news, I insist you take self-defense courses, and I'll take them with you to verify you've properly earned your bruises."

That told me one thing: Kenneth was a chip off my father's block, and unless I was careful, I'd be stuck with a fourth overprotective idiot.

This is going to be a disaster.

I SHOULD'VE STOLEN a pillow from our room so I could nap through the explanation on the various forms of dances and what we'd be learning, which included a smattering of everything. I looked forward to the flamenco. Unlike ballet, which focused on grace, beauty, and art, flamenco focused on the passion and love of dance with a flair I loved.

Some days, I regretted there was so little flamenco in my life.

At the forty-minute mark, the primary instructor, Danny Woolwright, picked up two ceramic jars and set them on a display table at the front of the room. "Partner assignments will be done by random draw. You will work with the same partner for the entirety of the week. This is an excellent chance to get used to working with someone new. I will draw a name from a jar. When I do, the person I name will come to the front and draw from the other jar. This way, no one can accuse me of rigging the pairings. You choose your own fate. Any questions?"

Silence.

"This is going to be a disaster," Kenneth predicted in a whisper. "Whoever does the drawing will probably be blamed for poor partnerships."

Considering how many beauties were in the room, at least thirty who outshined me in all ways possible, it'd be a recipe for competition and strife. Even if I pulled out all the stops and wore makeup and tried to be more of a swan, I'd resemble a goose next to the other participants, Kenneth included. Being the daughter of a succubus hadn't graced me with beauty. I fell in around average, which was all I needed. Makeup could hide my imperfections when needed. "You're probably right."

Mr. Woolwright dipped his hand into the first jar, pulled out a slip of paper, and called the name of a prima ballerina from a Russian company so out of my league I slouched in my seat. I'd heard rumors about Polina Romanovna Lebedintseva, and I pitied the man partnered with her.

Her standards went far beyond the sane, which factored into why she was a prima ballerina. I wasn't.

She glided to the front of the room, and at the instructor's nod, she dipped her hand into the other jar, pulled out a name, and announced, "Branko Herceg."

I hadn't heard of the young man, but I bet every other woman in the room envied Polina; he wore a black leotard, and he'd forgone the traditional codpiece.

Kenneth leaned towards me. "No one told me this was a pornography audition."

I clamped my lips together so I wouldn't laugh.

"You two will be partnered together, so please sit together and introduce yourselves."

The pair picked seats near the front, and Polina wasted no time chatting with her new partner.

Mr. Woolwright plucked a piece of paper from the men's jar and called Kenneth's name.

I wished him the best of luck. He'd need it, especially if he partnered with someone like Polina, who could dance circles around everyone else in the room.

He took his sweet time strolling to the front, and a woman slid into the seat he'd just left. "You know that man?"

As I wasn't ready to tell anyone the truth about him, I faked a laugh and shrugged. "He's an acquaintance who works with my father."

"He's not your partner?"

"Nope."

Kenneth dipped his hand into the women's jar and plucked out a piece of paper. He chuckled and said, "Emma Sansaul."

I bowed my head, groaned, and wondered how the hell he could've drawn my name when there was still twenty to thirty other women in the room. "Damn it."

Rising to my feet, I exhaled and strode to the front of the room, wondering how it was possible I'd have to dance with him and share his room for a week. The first person I'd blame would be Ma. Angels could manipulate random draws, I bet. They could teleport, become invisible at will, and ran around without a head.

Manipulating a few sheets of paper wasn't beyond Ma's abilities.

"Go introduce yourselves and have a seat," our instructor ordered.

Kenneth smirked. "After you."

As his seat was still occupied by the dark-haired woman

who'd asked me about Kenneth, I nodded towards the pair who'd already been selected. "I think you have a fan."

"Oh?"

"That woman came over and asked how I knew you. I told her you were an acquaintance who worked with my father."

"I like your use of the truth."

Of course. He was an FBI agent. Like angels, they probably hated when people lied to them. I bet it happened all the time in his line of work. "I just thought you'd like to know."

"Well, I do. I know her."

I hated reality sometimes. "Jealous girlfriend?"

"She's a drug addict and dealer I busted a few years back. She landed in rehab for six months. I'm surprised she picked up something like dancing."

"It's good exercise."

"Cathy was pretty vocal about why she got into dealing. She was too lazy to get a real job and liked getting people hooked on what only she could provide. Don't let her trick you. She's the type of predator that doesn't stop being a predator because she got caught."

"Wonderful. You know the most charming people."

"It's not all bad. I got to bust you, jail bird."

"Just be glad I didn't have to go to court. My dad would've eaten you and Mom alive. Then again, I'm regretting that the case didn't. I bet you would've run away when you found out who my father was."

"I find that unlikely. He enjoys every chance he gets to spank me in court. It's one of his joys in life, I'm convinced of it. And anyway, you didn't have to go to court because you wisely asked for an angel to confirm you had no idea it was an illegal substance. You just thought it was standard-grade pixie dust. That angel wasn't your ma, right?"

"No, it wasn't. Mom told me to deal with it myself without crying to Ma." The truth was a little harsher, and it involved being grounded for life if I took shortcuts trying to figure out how to get myself out of jail because I needed to be an adult without relying on my parents.

I'd been in law school long enough to learn exactly how to get myself out of such situations, and I'd done so without batting an eye. The pixie dust had factored in getting myself out of solitary with only a minimal desire to murder my own mother for landing me in prison for a night.

Had the neutralizer worked on the first dose, I would've been home within a few hours of arrest.

"Most parents would just make them pay the bills and get a job."

"I figured that part out fine on my own. Mom decided Dad's methods were too tame."

"Well, she is a succubus. They love causing trouble whenever possible, and since she can't cause the sort of trouble she'd normally cause, I bet she used you as an outlet."

"Or it was part of some elaborate scheme to hook me up with someone in law enforcement to make Dad happy," I muttered.

"That would be quite the scheme. I busted you years ago. Would she really try to hook you up with a random law enforcement officer?"

"Yes. She tried to bring home an incubus for me so I would miss my flight here. I'm pretty sure she wasn't planning on me keeping the incubus, but she's a firm believer in a woman's right to sleep with however many men she wants, when she wants, and how she wants. She keeps forgetting I'm infected with lycanthropy."

"Or she recognizes you'd have to go to extreme lengths to infect someone."

"True." I shrugged. "Welcome to my life."

"What was the deal with that Polina woman, anyway? He called her name, and you deflated."

"She's a Russian prima ballerina, one of the best in the industry. There are a lot of big league dancers here, and I'm in the minors comparatively."

"But you're a professional dancer."

"That doesn't mean I'm in the same class as they are."

"I have trouble believing that."

I arched a brow at him, shook my head, and watched the instructor partner dancers together for the rest of the week. The process took less than ten minutes, leaving us with a short window to head to the grand hall, where we'd spend the vast majority of our time learning new dance techniques. Inevitably, the prima ballerinas would compete among each other to be considered the best dancer of the retreat, something I viewed as idiotic.

I rose from my seat and stretched, waiting for the other pairs to file out of the room. Kenneth followed my lead.

Sharing a flight with him had been one thing. Cohabiting in the same suite had been another.

A week of him putting his hands all over me while we figured out how to perform new dance techniques as a pairing went above and beyond. He tested me in more ways than I liked.

Of all the shitty things to happen, why had I been busted by a handsome law enforcement officer? Had Mom not sabotaged my foray into pixie dust usage with the highest-grade stuff she could get her filthy hands on and brought him home instead of an incubus, I might've been tempted into doing the sorts of things she wanted me to do. Under no circumstances could I let my parents learn about that.

They'd join forces and take it further than Ma's attempts to bribe him with a dowry.

I could be a professional. I'd done it many times before. Part of my job as a dancer was to deal with my partner handling me so we could get through the performance. Some of the men overly enjoyed some of the more sexual elements of dancing, but most just did their job and worried about getting through the performance without making mistakes.

Applying the same professionalism to the retreat would get me through it.

Him testing my restraint hadn't been in the cards. Him being at the retreat at all hadn't been in the cards.

What had happened to my relaxing vacation? All I'd wanted was to have a good time and learn something while I did it.

Cathy dragged her new partner over to us before we had a chance to escape, and the poor man already looked like he wanted to be anywhere else. "You have all the luck, Emma," she announced with a glare promising I'd landed right on her shit list for something I hadn't even done.

I needed to stop thinking things couldn't get worse. They could always somehow get worse. One day, I would learn this most important lesson. I pointed at Kenneth. "He did the picking. I'm just the poor bastard stuck with him."

That caught her off guard. "Stuck with him?"

"He's my father's unpaid babysitter, and I'm willing to bet he'll report every single one of my sins to my family, resulting in hell for the next six months if I stumble once during a routine." To make it clear what I thought of the situation, I rolled my eyes and turned my worst glare on Kenneth. "In case you've forgotten, sir, I am an adult."

He played along, arched a brow, and matched me glare for glare. "I'm sure you think you're an adult."

"You really aren't with him?" Something in Cathy's tone changed, and her expression softened. "I thought you were a couple. I'm Cathy."

"We're not a couple."

Yet. If Ma had her way, we would be, and Mom would join in because she was itching for another child. Dad would follow my mothers' lead, as he was a lycanthrope and lived to add more chicks to the family. That my mothers had quelled his desire for more chicks with baby chickens would forever amuse me.

Had I gotten a say in the matter, I'd have at least two younger siblings to torture and use as distractions, yet another secret Ma likely knew because she couldn't help but poke her nose into my business at her whim.

Damned angels.

When I was honest with myself, I'd probably side with my mothers in the whole Kenneth fiasco.

"Huh. I thought you were older." Cathy beamed at Kenneth. "It's been a while."

"Cathy," he greeted.

I'd been around him long enough to catch a hint of wariness in his tone. Wouldn't someone who'd gone through rehab be the type of person he admired? Why would she, who looked unhealthily thin but nothing outside the realm of normal for a dancer, make him wary?

I suspected it had something to do with his work.

"I didn't think you were a dancer."

"It's a hobby. I needed to take some time off work, and this looked interesting, so I signed up. I passed the minimum requirements, so here I am. As I'm not a professional, I had to meet with Mr. Woolwright privately for an evaluation and work on some skills."

"Huh. Didn't know they let the amateurs in here."

"When did you become a professional?"

Cathy flushed. "I joined a troupe earlier this year."

"Good for you. I thought it'd take a lot longer for your knees and ankles to handle strenuous workouts."

Cooked lobsters had nothing on Cathy's face. "It's wasn't like that. I blitzed through physical therapy."

I'd seen enough dancers cave to anorexia attempting to fit society's standards. Some of the women still fought it years later, their bones too brittle to keep dancing despite intensive physical therapy aided with magic. I'd stood in for a prima ballerina once; she'd been in traction for a terrifying period of time trying to preserve her knee so she could keep dancing.

It'd taken her a year and a half to recover enough to return to the stage. I doubted I'd ever stand-in for another prima ballerina in my career, such as it was, but the incident had taught me a few important lessons: everyone had secrets, everyone had challenges and hardships, and everyone fell.

"Congratulations."

"Do you think we'll really be stuck with the same partner for the entire week?"

"It seems likely to me." Kenneth shrugged, turning to Cathy's partner and holding out his hand. "I'm Kenneth."

I'd seen plenty of men exchange handshakes in my life, but I got the sense of mutual suffering from the pair. I wanted to join them in solidarity, expecting Cathy would go out of her way to make my life miserable because Kenneth had drawn my name instead of hers.

So much for my nice vacation.

"We better get to the main hall before we're late," I said, and without waiting to see if they listened, headed for the door, thinking curses Ma would clean my mouth out over if she heard them.

She took me wishing anyone a quick trip to hell seriously, probably because I had enough demonic blood in me to make such a thing feasible. It wasn't like I was the devil's daughter. That honor fell to some other poor bastard, and I wished her the best of luck dealing with her adoptive parents.

I marched towards the main hall, chin lifted high and determined to salvage something of my week, even if it meant allowing myself to enjoy every single flub while dancing with Kenneth—another thought I couldn't afford to let Ma hear.

I needed to figure out how to safeguard my thoughts from an angel before my own mother killed me in retribution for having a smidgeon too much of Mom in me. The crowd ahead in the hallway ensured I'd be late getting to my destination, yet another black mark on my day, but then I realized they were all dancers, and something ahead held their attention.

Sometimes, I enjoyed being tall, willowy, and light on my feet; it made it easier to stand on my toes and peek over the heads of those in front of me.

A woman's body hung from the ceiling, her body spinning in a slow circle. She looked a lot like me and had been dead long enough her eyes were clouded over. A sickly sweet stench hung in the air, and something dripped from dark plastic dangling from the broken ceiling tiles overhead.

I covered my mouth with my hands and hoped I wouldn't throw up.

Kenneth touched my elbow, and I pointed at the woman, my hand shaking.

"Another one," he murmured, his eyes narrowing. He reached into his pocket, retrieved his phone, and sent a text message to someone. "She's at least a day old judging from the state of decomposition, probably closer to two. Depends on what temperature she was stored at before she was put there."

I wasn't sure I wanted to know why he knew so much about bodies.

As though able to listen to my thoughts like Ma, he added, "I've done the violent crimes circuit a time or two, and it's not uncommon in drug overdoses for it to take a few days for the victim to be found."

I swallowed several times before whispering, "I'm starting to think what happened in the pool yesterday wasn't an accident, Kenneth."

"I'm starting to think you're right."

Cathy and her unfortunate partner joined us, and when she caught sight of the body, she screamed.

I needed a new life, a bottle of the hardest liquor I could get my hands on, and a vacation from my vacation.

SEVEN

You're on the case.

A HERD of police officers arrived within ten minutes, half of them beelined for the body while the rest went straight for Kenneth like a pack of vultures after an easy meal. Had I been wiser, I would've taken my chance to escape while I could.

The lead vulture whipped out his badge and barked, "Chief Rochester. Are you Agent Bernard?"

"I am. If you want to see my badge, I'll need to go to my room." I envied Kenneth's pockets, which had enough room for his wallet and phone. He dug out his driver's license and held it out for the officer's inspection. "How can I help you?"

"You're on the case."

What the hell? So much for hoping for happy little accidents on the dance floor. At the rate we were going, we wouldn't be doing any dancing at all.

Kenneth sucked in a breath, his gaze locking on the woman's body, which continued to spin in slow, gruesome circles. "What? Why? I'm in the narcotics department."

"Congratulations. You've been reassigned to murder investigations in Colorado until further notice." The police chief grunted, turned to the body, and shook his head. "Yesterday's death has been officially classified as a murder."

"And this case is being bumped to me why? Murder investigations are the domain of local law enforcement."

While tempted, I didn't remind Kenneth local law enforcement could request an FBI agent at any time to aid with an investigation, especially if there was reason to believe the case would cross state lines or involve a Federal felony.

"We'll discuss this in private. You've been authorized to bring in one assistant for the duration of the investigation, as I've been notified you don't have an active partner and have been working undercover for the past few months. It's a special exemption, and your assistant will be paid a standard fee for the work."

Kenneth glanced at me. "Up for some paperwork and taking notes, Emma?"

I bowed my head, sighed, and waved goodbye to my sane, quiet life. "Sure. Why not? It's not like I had anything else to do this week."

He snorted. "I know that feeling. All right. We both need to get changed, then we're going to need to be briefed. I'm also going to need to know who authorized the involvement of a civilian assistant, the court order allowing it, and appropriate waivers from the FBI."

"We're drawing up the documentation you need, and you'll have it within the next hour. We were going to wait until later this afternoon to involve you, but our timetable has been moved up. Paulson and Alwins? Go with them," Chief Rochester ordered.

A pair of cops overdue for retirement stepped forward and waited, offering Kenneth solemn nods. Officer Paulson had more gray in his hair than brown, and Officer Alwins seemed to have given up the war against his receding hairline with good cheer, polishing the bald top of his head to a shine.

Kenneth gave me a gentle push in the general direction of the elevators. I dodged Cathy and her partner, eager to escape the crowd gawking at the deceased woman and the cops who'd already begun the process of pulling people aside to question them about the gruesome discovery. Accepting I wouldn't be dancing would make the rest of the week easier to get through, although I'd be having a long talk with Kenneth about why he wanted me to help him.

As far as he knew, I knew nothing about bodies, law enforcement, or anything he might view as useful. I wondered if Ma considered investigating a chain of suspicious deaths at a resort as a promotion.

Angels cheated when they could, sneaking peeks into the inevitable future. Sometimes, they worked to ensure the future they wanted came to fruition. Other times, they watched the fireworks because mortals amused them.

We made the trip to our room in silence, and both cops arched a brow when Kenneth unlocked the door.

"Her room was double booked at the hotel, so I offered to share. Her father is an attorney I see often enough in court, so we're acquainted."

The cops relaxed, and Office Paulson chuckled. "I'd wondered why you'd pick a civ for your assistant instead of calling in someone. An attorney's daughter would know some of the tricks of the trade."

I was tempted to wield my JD as a weapon and beat some cops and an FBI agent with it.

"I don't know what self-deprecating thought is rattling around in your head, jail bird, but stop it," Kenneth ordered. "And no, I didn't pick you because of your mothers."

I bowed my head and groaned. "Why couldn't you need help with a court transcription? I could do that."

"Jail bird?" Officer Alwins asked. "Wait. Mothers?"

"My father's a lycanthrope, mother number one is an angel, and mother number two is a succubus," I explained. "He probably wants me to ask Ma to verify the truth so he doesn't have to put up with a bunch of bureaucratic bullshit. He's supposed to be on vacation."

"What can you tell me?" Kenneth asked, tossing his wallet and phone on the coffee table before heading towards his bedroom to change. I took the hint and headed for my bag, closing the door so I could put something on more appropriate for pretending I was qualified to help Kenneth do anything. Within five minutes, I'd changed into jeans and the nicest blouse I had with me, hoping it'd be acceptable.

The cops were waiting in the living room, their attention glued to their smartphones. When Kenneth finally emerged, he was dressed in a suit and had a firearm holstered at his hip. I pointed at it and blurted, "How the hell did you get that on the plane?"

"It went in my checked baggage. I might've been able to get a cabin carry permit, but they're a pain in the ass to get on a good day."

"What do you want me to do?"

Kenneth tossed me a notepad and a pen. "You get to take notes. Note who we talk to, why we're talking to them, anything important they know, anything that stands out to you, and otherwise anything I tell you to write down. We'll compare notes when we're done and see if we can figure out who is killing women. More importantly, we'll try to figure out who might be the next victim, but I have a few ideas I don't like."

"From what I've seen, they match my general description. But why would someone target women at a resort like this?"

"Your guess is as good as mine right now. Please tell me this is a temporary position until someone with the right skillset comes in to replace me." Kenneth stared at the cops, and they both shook their heads. "This is going to be a disaster. I've worked in violent crimes and narcotics. That does not make me qualified to handle what might turn out to be a serial killer."

"That's what I said when I got promoted to detective," Officer Alwins replied. "It's nice to see the FBI chaps have the same issues we do."

Kenneth eyed his phone and dialed a number. "Hey, boss? I thought I was supposed to be on vacation."

I wished I could hear the other end of the conversation. Kenneth's expression transformed from annoyed to incredulous, then he blurted, "Have you lost your mind?"

I blinked, as did the cops.

"Won't he get fired for saying something like that to his boss? I would. I bet your chief would kick your asses if you took that tone with him. He looks like the ass-kicker type."

The cops nodded.

"Am I the only one who thinks this is an incredibly bad idea? Not just incredibly bad, it's the dumbest damned thing I've heard of in my life. Are you trying to create a disaster?" Kenneth grunted and held the phone out to me. "Talk to him before I smash my phone, please."

"What the fuck is wrong with you? I'm not talking to your boss!"

"Talk to him. Please. Don't make me beg."

Technically, he was already begging, but I let him get away with it, huffed, and snatched the cell out of his hand and put it to my ear. "Hello, Emma Sansaul speaking."

"Weston Harold. You've been recruited," a deep voice informed me. I classified the bastard on the other end as overly smug and in dire need of an attitude adjustment.

"Well, that was an incredibly stupid thing to do. I thought qualifications mattered in the FBI. I'm assuming I'm talking to someone in the FBI? Unless you need a ballerina, I don't see how I am of any use to you."

"Let's begin with your criminal law degree, Dr. Sansaul."

Crap. "What criminal law degree?" I asked, and had I been meeting with the man face-to-face, my ship would've been sunk, as I had an unfortunate tendency to look away from someone when trying to lie. I already regretted having agreed to sit through the bar exam and deal with all the damned paperwork and schooling to get my JD, something I refused to use and pretended didn't exist whenever possible. The agreement had been in stone, and I'd used the loophole ruthlessly: I got the JD and maintained my license, and Dad wouldn't complain about my dancing. No one said I had to practice law beyond the minimums to maintain my license, and I'd taken every dance and arts course I could get my greedy hands on while pursuing his dream job for me.

I'd become the family pride and disappointment in one fell swoop, and true to our agreement, Dad didn't complain I'd chosen to dance rather than join him in lawyering.

"You have a criminal law degree?" Kenneth asked.

Busted. I scowled at him and waved him off.

"I have your license, issued in New York, sitting on my desk. You're quite an intelligent individual, Ms. Sansaul, Esquire. It's a shame such talent and education aren't being used."

Which one of my parents would die first? Ma would pose the biggest challenge; the immortality thing put kinks in any plans to kill her off. I'd have to concoct a special hell for my father, who was the most likely culprit in this ploy aimed at involving me with the FBI. "I was arrested once, by Agent Bernard. That should disqualify me from any form of law enforcement."

It didn't, especially as I'd been cleared of all charges without the incident being put on my permanent record.

"You were an unwitting victim of a prank by one of your mothers, verified under oath by an angel. That doesn't disqualify you."

Well, shit. Mr. Harold had done his homework, probably with some help from my traitorous parents. "How about the triple homicide of my parents? Would that disqualify me? If you could excuse me, I'll go hunt the bastards down and start adding to the fucking bodies in this hotel!"

Kenneth's boss laughed at me. "That does fit well with your field of study. From my understanding, you have an interest in prosecuting murder cases. Partnering with Agent Bernard on a trial basis before attending proper training, scheduled to begin within a month upon signing of your hiring agreement, would be an excellent way to pursue those interests. Agent Bernard will need a partner in his new field and partnering him with a strong analytical thinker would be ideal. You'd also be able to advise him on legal matters to limit mistakes that might cost the prosecution."

"Do I look like I want this job?"

"My opening offer is an eighty-three thousand a year, full health benefits, a flexible schedule to allow for you to continue dancing in some capacity, and any expanded education and training you require."

I froze. Eight-three thousand a year was far more than I made, and while I could've made more as an attorney following in my father's footsteps, having a flexible schedule allowing me to dance would work well with my goal to escape my parents for good. "Define flexible."

"Unless you're on an active case requiring time-sensitive action, you would be able to pursue your personal interests. It's a benefit of specializing within the FBI. Of course, specialization within the violent crimes department isn't without risks, especially as serial killers are a special breed of cat, but when an opportunity presents itself, it's difficult to ignore it. Agent Bernard is wasted in narcotics, and with your physical conditioning and intellect, I think you'll be a good match for him."

"Which one of my asshole parents put you up to this? I need to best decide how to start my career as a serial killer," I hissed. Drawing a deep breath, I filled my lungs, held it until my chest burned, and exhaled in a long sigh. "I'd like to remind you I'm an infected lycanthrope. Doesn't that disqualify me from work in law enforcement?"

"No, it doesn't. We have special exemptions for instances like this. Our file on you shows a low contagion risk, although I've been informed it's probable you'll infect Agent Bernard. With your slow development of a contagious virus, we're unconcerned. It would take catastrophic injury likely resulting in death for there to be any significant risk of infection to the general public. As your virus levels mature, we may take steps to limit the chance of infection, but you're not a predatory species."

Did Kenneth's boss know nothing about swans? "No, we're just grouchy and prone to attacking whatever moves because we're assholes."

Instead of being properly concerned, he laughed again. "I've been briefed on the aggressive tendencies of swans. Please consider this as an opportunity to evaluate this as a potential career path. It took me all night to get the appropriate waivers and permissions to add you to this case as a civilian."

I bet my father had instructed Kenneth's boss to use that line on me. "Tell me which one of my parents is behind this travesty so I can begin my career as a serial killer, and I'll grudgingly accept your proposal. As my vacation is being ruined, I'll expect compensation."

"How does a new vacation sound? I believe we can get an instructor of the appropriate qualifications to work with you and a partner for a week. I recommend Agent Bernard. He does have rudimentary dance training."

"Agent Bernard might be victim number four, as he's considering accepting a dowry from Ma because he's an insufferable asshole."

"The FBI offers complementary anger management courses. We also have couples therapy for those who have bypassed the fraternization rules."

"I'm not going to win this one, am I?"

"I suspect not. I'd be foolish to let such an opportunity pass me by."

"I think it's more foolish you'd want me in this capacity in the first place."

"Perhaps so, but I think I will come out ahead on this gamble. Are you in?"

I sighed, cursed the day I'd wanted to go on a vacation, and shrugged. "Why the fuck not? I'll be expecting a full list of those responsible for this idiocy so they can be properly disciplined."

"It would make me an accomplice if I listed them by name, but I will state there were three involved in your current situation. Do give Agent Bernard the happy news on my behalf."

Kenneth's boss hung up, and I scowled, considering how best to deliver the so-called happy news. Shoving Kenneth's phone directly up his ass would send a message, but I wanted my opening act of violence to be against my parents. I wasn't sure which I'd target first.

Ma held the top spot as my first victim, as I'd be able to wear myself out and work through my rage long before I subdued her enough to do any lasting harm to Mom or Dad. I grunted and offered Kenneth his phone. "Someone thought it would be a good idea to recommend me as a candidate for the FBI. It turns out this someone is actually three someones, and I'll be starting my career as a serial killer with two counts of matricide and one count of patricide before I come after you for your unwitting involvement in this travesty."

"The first rule of becoming a serial killer involves not telling anyone you're going to become a serial killer, jail bird. You have two police officers as witnesses now. That's stupid."

"So is recruiting me for the FBI."

"He was really recruiting you?"

"And he guilt tripped me, saying he'd been working all night to get the appropriate paperwork to bring me in on this case on a trial basis."

"You know what? I'm just not going to ask. We'll deal with it later, after we figure out who is killing these women and why."

"Good plan. Hey, Kenneth?"

"What?"

"You'll help me hide the bodies, right?"

"Good lord, jail bird. Witnesses. You can't ask these questions in front of witnesses."

"So you would, except I'd have to ask you when there aren't witnesses? Because my parents need to die for this."

"One of your mothers is immortal, the other is a demon who'll be difficult to kill on a good day, and your father's a lycanthrope. I don't think you're going to have any bodies to bury without an intervention or a lot of help."

"Technically, an intervention is a lot of help."

"Just grab your purse and let's get going. You're not killing your parents."

"Today," I corrected. "I'm not killing them today, as it seems I have more important things to do."

"You know what? I'll take what I can get. We'll renegotiate about the fate of your parents tomorrow."

The cops exchanged looks and burst into laughter.

EIGHT

What did I do now?

I SPOTTED Dad in the lobby, grabbed the strap of my purse, and went in for the kill. I caught him by surprise, my first blow smacking him in the back of his thick skull. My second caught him across the cheek and snapped his head to the side. "You!"

He caught my wrist and put an end to his deserved beating. "What did I do now?"

"You contacted the FBI with my degree and bar exam results, you insufferable piece of shit!"

"Oh, that."

I didn't need my purse or my right hand to kill my father. My teeth would do just fine, and I still had my left hand. I snarled curses and went for his throat.

My bastard father caught my free hand and held me at arm's length, daring to laugh at me. "Nothing in our family agreement stated I couldn't use your degree or your bar exam results for your benefit. There was no NDA signed or promise of classification made for those records. Just like you got away with mooching a JD off me so you could spend the past five years dancing your little heart out at the theater, it's my turn to make full use the loopholes inherent in our agreement. I even negotiated a decent starting salary on your behalf. All you need to do is handle this investigation and sign to start your shiny, new career."

"Helicopter parent," I hissed through clenched teeth, kicking at his ankles. "This is not funny."

"Neither is the reality of several murdered women and a solo FBI agent here capable of handling the case. He needs a partner for safety purposes, and you meet the minimum requirements in untraditional fashions. It'll be a good learning experience and an excellent career choice for you. You're old enough you'd be losing your edge on the stage if it weren't for my lycanthropy virus."

"You're a cretin."

"I'm also right. As the safety angle is pretty bogus due to your utter inability to protect yourself, your mothers and I will be tagging along as helpful civilians."

While tempted to cry, I aimed another kick at his ankles. "You're going to pay for this."

A strong arm wrapped around my waist, lifted me off my feet, and hauled me away from my father. "All right, jail bird. We already talked about this. We'll negotiate about your parents tomorrow. We have work to do, and that work doesn't involve killing him."

Dad released my wrists. "They've moved the dancers to the main hall for general questioning; we thought it'd be helpful, so your mothers are there to encourage people to be honest."

"I can understand that with Ma. What's Mom doing in this except causing me more problems?"

"She's playing human and glaring on your ma's behalf."

"Ma doesn't need a head to glare at people, Dad. She just does it, and it's creepy."

"I know, I know. Just deal with it, Emma. Go help your new partner get this case closed."

"You act like this will be a quick process."

"Your mothers assured me it would be. They both noticed the victims look a lot like you, and neither like it. Honestly, you two probably won't have to do a thing with them on the warpath. I'm just staying out of the way and volunteering for the prosecution to keep my wives happy. It's tough keeping one of them happy, but when both are upset, things become very complicated for me. You should know this, Emma."

"It's your fault for marrying two women."

"They're a package set."

"And they want to kill each other on a bad day."

"They're the best sort of package set a man could ever ask for."

I twisted in Kenneth's arms to discover both of my mothers approaching. "You fiends."

Ma snorted. "I am no fiend."

"You sold me to the FBI!"

"No, I sold you to the FBI agent. I merely assisted the FBI in finding a new candidate for a specialized position."

Kenneth sighed. "I thought you were with the dancers for questioning."

"The questioning is being moved to the police station for general recording. We weren't invited. You two are expected at the body. Forensics found something you might be interested in. And Emma?"

"What, Ma?"

"Don't throw up on the body. That's a good way to ruin evidence."

"Thanks, Ma."

"Anytime, little chick. Run along. You have murders to solve. Do put that expensive schooling to use like a good girl."

Kenneth dragged me off before I could discover it was possible to murder an angel with my bare hands.

THE WOMAN'S body still hung from the ceiling, although someone had brought in a ladder to make it easier to reach her. A woman and a man in lab coats examined the area, and the instant we approached, Chief Rochester offered us a pair of gloves. I snapped mine on, my gaze locked on the woman's corpse.

Ma had teased me about throwing up on the body for a reason, and I'd make sure if I lost control of my stomach, I wouldn't ruin any evidence. The first time I'd done a forensics lab course, half the class had gotten sick during the first dissection of a human cadaver. I'd been one of them, and I'd suffered from nightmares for a week.

I gave the course a great deal of credit. It had numbed me to the presence of death. The week-long stint in a New York morgue had finished what the lab work hadn't. The longer I stared at her hanging from the ceiling, the more I realized my parents were right in some ways. I had the right education to do the job if I got off my ass and did it.

I inhaled, steeled my nerves, and started my inspection of her body at her throat where she hung. I expected the abrasion marks and bruising from the rope, but a second set of marks just above the noose captured my attention, and I pointed at her. "Looks like she was strangled before being hung."

"That's our current theory, although until we get her down, we're not going to be able to have a better look at her for additional evidence of trauma," Chief Rochester replied. "The strangulation marks are consistent to what we found on the woman's body in the swimming pool. The third victim, found overnight, may have also been strangled, but we won't have a confirmation until the coroner has a closer look at her. This one's unusual, as the body bag used to transport her is still here. We're not sure how the other bodies were transported."

Kenneth scowled, got up onto the ladder, and leaned towards the woman's body to get a closer look at the strangulation marks. "I don't see any scratch marks."

I dropped my gaze to the woman's hands. Unlike me, she kept her nails long, and I couldn't find a single flaw in the polish. Leaning over, I peeked at the nail bed. Despite the discoloration from blood and fluids pooling in her fingertips, I saw no evidence of abrasion or skin material from a struggle. "Her nails look clean."

As my job was to make Kenneth's job easier, I grabbed the notebook and went to work detailing the condition of the woman's body, the obvious marks of violence, possible causes of death, and everything else I could glean from her, careful to keep my breathing steady so I could control my churning stomach.

Lab work and time in the morgue hadn't made me completely immune to the realities of death.

To be safe rather than sorry, I stepped away from her

corpse, shaking my head that someone would so brutally end a life.

From everything I'd learned while pursuing my education, identifying the motivation could often lead to the killer, and evidence helped guide the way much like when someone used a flashlight to walk in the dark. Brown hair, a light tan, and fit, athletic women of moderate height left a lot of motivations to uncover.

If they all had dark blue eyes like mine, I'd be on the likely potential victim list, a disconcerting reality. For the case to be classified as the work of a serial killer, there had to be links to each death. The story their deaths told would, if Kenneth, the forensics team, and the police did their jobs right, lead to the killer.

As Kenneth's boss had said, serial killers were a different breed of cat from the average murderer, who often killed out of either greed or passion. I found it odd that flashes of rage so intense it cost someone their life were labeled as an act of passion.

Humans disgusted me sometimes.

Kenneth used the ladder to examine her from head to toe, and I dutifully took notes for his review later. When he got down, he sighed and shook his head. "Anyone have a look in the ceiling yet?"

"There's a body bag, and it looks like someone had put some form of acid on the rope that was holding her up there. The body bag was secured at several points in the ceiling, and she was held up there with several ropes, which show acid damage as far as we can tell. Until we get the labs back, we won't know for certain."

"Get her down from there," Kenneth ordered.

I retreated, mindful of Ma's advice and my past experiences in the morgue.

Kenneth joined me, his expression grim. "I'd rather be dancing."

I stared at the woman's feet. A pair of classic black Mary Janes with kitten heels wouldn't be my first choice of dance shoe, but I'd seen similar worn by tap dancers. I frowned, approached the body again, and got on my hands and knees for a closer look at the sole.

Unlike a typical shoe, tap dancers had special metal pads on the soles to make the sounds unique to their performance style. I scowled and pointed at what I'd discovered. "She's wearing tap dancing shoes. We might want to find out if any of the dancers didn't show up to the retreat, Kenneth."

Something cold and wet dripped down the back of my neck, and thanks to Ma's warning I shouldn't puke on the corpse, I scrambled away from the body, shudders tearing through me. Compulsive swallowing kept my stomach under control, and I closed my eyes, drew in a shaky breath, and questioned every decision I'd made in my life.

I GAVE the forensics people credit; they were thorough in their collection of evidence and cleaning my back, as they were worried the acid responsible for snapping the ropes in the ceiling had transferred to my skin. Fortunately, I emerged unharmed, although I reeked of disinfectant.

"You handled that a lot better than I expected," Kenneth admitted.

"Despite appearances and my job as a dancer, I took a lot

of classes to augment my field of specialty. It kept Dad from whining. After I finished my classes, it seemed like a waste to dodge the bar exam, so I took it, and I maintain my license since I don't feel like completely wasting his investment. But honestly, it took those years of schooling to realize I don't really want to be a lawyer *or* a professor."

"That's a really expensive way to learn you don't want a job."

"I tried to tell that to Dad after my third year in, but at that point, he'd already paid for three years of college, so I kept my mouth shut and finished."

"Yet you went beyond the basics you needed to qualify to take your bar exam."

"Angelic disappointment is a terrible thing. You try telling Ma you have a perfect GPA but don't want to actually be a lawyer. She might not have a head, but she's really good at hamming up the parental heartbreak. Mom was the one who suggested I take the extra time and pick a minor I liked to get through the schooling. That's how I got into dancing."

"You're not really good at rebellion, are you?"

"I figured it out eventually. Mostly."

"This really isn't your first time dealing with bodies, is it?"

"The trick to lying without actually lying is failing to confirm the truth. You assumed I've never been around bodies before, and I allowed you to maintain your initial impression as I try not to think too much about the number of bodies I've observed in labs or at the morgue. I'd taken the labs to help build better prosecution cases in murder trials, as I figured if I had the same skill sets as lab techs and detectives, I might be able to present the puzzle in such a way the killers wouldn't be able to mount good defenses against the presented evidence."

"Just how many labs have you taken?"

"Don't ask. I took the minimum criminal law classes required for my degrees and filled out the rest of my requirements with labs. I crammed in every elective I could for the arts and dancing on the side. Scheduling was a bitch, and I took the maximum allowed number of courses every semester."

"And held the top position for your class."

"As I said, infection with the lycanthropy virus doesn't mean we're stupid."

"No wonder my boss is itching to get a hold of you. He usually has to pick from law enforcement wanting more from their careers."

I shrugged. "What's our next step?"

"We get the victims identified, get a complete list of everyone registered for the dance retreat, and find out if our Jane Does were supposed to be attending. If so, we start looking into who might want to kill a bunch of dancers and why. If we're lucky, we'll get DNA evidence pointing to the killer, but I'm not going to hold my breath."

"For someone from the narcotics department, you know a lot about the procedures for handling murder cases."

"I told you I've done work in the violent crimes division."

"So why would your boss view you as wasted in narcotics? Didn't he assign you there?"

"No. I requested to be transferred." Kenneth's expression soured. "I don't want to talk about it."

Enlightenment struck me like a bolt of lightning, and I wondered at the circumstances. Something had happened to him in the field, but what?

I could make a few guesses, and his choice to join the narcotics team, which would fight daily to save lives from drug overdoses and addiction, led me to the same place. He'd been hunting for a killer and hadn't gotten to the victim on time, and he blamed himself for the death.

Hunting serial killers would put him back in those old, worn shoes. "A killer beat you."

He flinched. "It happens in this line of work."

"Let me guess: you made a mistake you feel cost someone their life, so you moved into narcotics, which likely has a high rate of deaths from overdose."

Kenneth glared at me but said nothing.

"I don't have a psychology degree, so I can't really help you with those issues, but if your boss is relying on a lycanthrope who can't even shift to kick you in the ass and get you back to work, I can do that. If I have to put up with this, so do you. Do whatever it is you FBI agent types do so I can get back to dancing."

He snorted. "Keep holding onto your delusions there, jail bird. I know my boss. He'll annoy you into doing what he wants, and if that doesn't work, he'll trick you into it."

"So I gathered. He's already scheduled me for training."

"Good luck escaping him. You're going to need it."

Mr. Woolwright did not like handing over the registration list for the dance retreat, and when Kenneth asked for the list of those who hadn't made the cut, hadn't shown up, or otherwise were missing, he demanded a warrant for the information.

It took Kenneth two phone calls and less than an hour to

get a warrant for the documentation. The dance instructor stared at the papers. The moment it sank in there was a real murder investigation going on involving his retreat, the man turned whiter than my ma's wings.

In addition to the list of attendants, Mr. Woolwright provided us with a list of all applications, no-shows, and cancellations. Armed with the information, we returned to our suite, and our coffee table became a war zone.

Kenneth called Chief Rochester with the names of four women who hadn't showed up for the retreat and their contact information, requesting that someone call and verify their whereabouts. He feared he knew where three of them were already, but without the databases he only had access to at work, he couldn't be certain.

I worried he was right, and if he was, it meant trouble.

On paper, we were interchangeable. We all had brown hair, were of similar build and age, and fit the same profile, adding weight to the idea it was the work of a serial killer.

But why would a serial killer target a dance retreat? If it was a deliberate targeting of dancers, there had to be something more to them than hair color, build, and age.

I scowled at the papers scattered over the coffee table. "Can we get information on these women? Their work history, dance specializations, or similar?"

"That depends on a lot of factors, including if we can contact them. If the information is determined to be a requirement for the investigation, we'll get a court order to have records pulled on each of them. If they're our victims, we'll be able to get the information without much effort; it'll all be classified as a part of the investigation by default and used for evidence and the identification of other potential victims."

I pointed at myself. "I fit the bill so far."

"I was trying not to think about that, honestly. The last thing I need is an infuriated lycanthrope rampaging because some idiot serial killer went after his daughter, and if the information on your card is accurate, your virus isn't robust enough to protect you from much."

I shrugged. "If we're looking at the patterns, I fit the pattern. We don't have to like it, we just need to accept it's probable. Unfortunately, probably half the women in attendance are our build. A lot prefer to dye their hair away from brown, though."

"That still leaves us with several women, yourself included, who match the pattern thus far. You don't tap dance, do you?"

"No, I don't."

"That's something, but not something I'm willing to gamble on."

"Trust me, I don't want to be stuffed in a ceiling and hung. Why would someone stuff someone in a ceiling and design it so she fell out after a while? How is it no one caught this person in the act?"

"That is a very good question." Kenneth grabbed his phone and dialed a number. "Sorry to bother you again, Chief Rochester, but have we gotten any information from the resort security about the three incidents? The pool should've had surveillance."

Kenneth listened, jotting a few notes and shaking his head. "All right. Give me a call when you have an update. Right now, we're trying to establish probable motives, but until we can get an ID on the bodies, it's guesswork. If the resort gives you any pushback on the security recordings, I'll go downstairs and crack some heads together. There's no reason they shouldn't have had those for you unless they need time to doctor them. I'll give a few contacts in the CDC a call if I need to get to the bottom of this."

I waited until Kenneth set his phone back on the coffee table to ask, "What happened to the recordings?"

"They're dragging their feet about it. I'll probably have to get another court order to get them to hand an unaltered copy over. Their security team is supposed to be monitoring the pool; there were no warning signs stating the area wasn't unmonitored, which might make them liable depending on the cause of the lapse and how the murder was committed. My bets are on strangulation using a cord of some sort. That leads me to believe the killer is a woman."

"Not strong enough to strangle someone with her bare hands?" I speculated.

"Correct, and the gouges on the woman's throat weren't deep enough to be consistent with a man's strength. While the killer could be a weak man or a man trying to hide his gender, I find it unlikely."

"But how would a woman haul someone into the ceiling like that without anyone noticing?"

"I'd place my bets on a pulley system of some sort, but we need to wait until everything has been documented and filed as evidence before we can try to replicate it."

"Can we try a different spot down the hallway as an experiment?"

"We can go down and ask if they found any evidence a pulley was used and see what else they've scrounged up while we've been up here going through this information." Kenneth gathered the papers, set them in his briefcase, and locked it. "Here's the first rule of investigating with me as your partner. We lock up all evidence in the most secure places we can and take it with us whenever possible. If I don't have a secure place, I head to the nearest police station and use one of their safes. I'm considered paranoid, but if the wrong person gets a hold of the information I'm working with, it can cause problems with the investigation."

"And let the guilty parties get ahead of us. Makes sense. No handing over anything to anyone, since we don't know what abilities someone might have, either."

"Well, you're ahead of the curve. The last individuals my boss tried to partner me with found me a little too paranoid for their liking."

"Why do I have a feeling part of the reason you've been solo undercover in narcotics is because you're such a pain in the ass that not even hardened FBI agents can handle you?"

"At risk of being assaulted by an aggressive, angry swan, you're smarter than you look."

I planted my hands on my hips. "And what is that supposed to mean?"

"If you decided to take up a career in pole dancing, you'd make a fortune. You're not society's standard bimbo, but you're packing the goods in a way that makes men pay attention. I'm blaming your mother for that, for the record."

Damned Mom, daring to pass some of her succubus genes to me. "I think you need your eyes examined, Kenneth."

"No, I don't. My eyes are just fine. I'll enjoy proving you're wrong. It'll be enjoyable for one of us."

Killing Kenneth wouldn't do; he needed to live a long time so I could pop his smug little bubble at my leisure. "You just love yanking my chain, don't you?"

"It's quickly becoming my favorite hobby."

Of course. I should've known. One day, I might understand Kenneth and his weird sense of humor. With the way my luck was headed, I'd end up stuck with him for a long time. At the rate I was going, I'd like it.

I blamed Dad and inheriting his virus for that. Lycanthropes liked a challenge. However, just to be sure, I'd ask Ma if I'd been dropped on my head as a baby. That might explain a few things, too.

NINE

Would a stash of busted security cameras interest you?

Progress had been made since we'd retreated to our room to talk about the situation. The woman was gone and several people were on ladders examining where her body had been hidden. Kenneth observed for a while before clearing his throat to catch their attention, soft enough he wouldn't startle someone into falling. "Got anything for us up there?"

"Would a stash of busted security cameras interest you?" one replied, climbing down with a plastic bag containing a broken mess of wires and plastic. The middle-aged man, his dark hair peppered with gray, nodded to me before focusing on Kenneth. "I think we've figured out why security didn't see anything in the pool. We've got at least twenty individual camera units up here. Looks like someone was in a hurry and needed a place to dump the evidence. We'll check for latent prints in the lab; it should be the first thing we have back for you."

"Any evidence of a pulley system up there?"

The man's brows rose. "Have you been down there waiting that long?"

"Not quite. We were trying to figure out how the killer got her up there."

"Well, you figured right. Someone jury-rigged a pulley system to one of the support beams up here. Shoddy but functional job. I got some useful information for you, though. Even more useful than the pulley, I think."

Kenneth stared up into the ceiling, his eyes narrowed in thought. "What did you find?"

"Someone used an aversion on the pool, the dumpster where the third body was found, and this hallway, and we think we have it timed out to lasting an hour and a half, plenty of time to knock out the cameras and keep anyone from coming to investigate. We'll have better information on the times of death by morning. Also, I'm confident all three victims were strangled and relocated after death. We believe the killer used aversions strategically placed in the building to hide the movement of the bodies, although I don't think the bodies were dragged to their destination. Unless we can recover something from the cameras, we may not be able to confirm how the bodies were moved unless we get a lucky break."

"Or the killer made a dumb mistake. Considering you've already found the cameras, I'm uncharacteristically hopeful." Kenneth gestured to the ladder. "You mind?"

The man pointed at a box of latex gloves tossed off to the side. "Look but don't touch. I've got a full set of photographs for you, which I'll upload within the next hour. The chief will send you the credentials to access them."

"Excellent." Kenneth snatched a pair of gloves, snapped

them on, and scrambled up the ladder to have a closer look in the ceiling. "What the hell? It's a dumpster up here!"

"Gathering evidence has been an adventure." The man flashed a grin at me. "Welcome aboard, ma'am. I'm Trevor, and I'm in charge of this motley crew of forensics gophers here to help you make sense of the senseless."

"Emma."

"If you call her jail bird, she bristles nicely," Kenneth added.

"You're lucky you're near evidence, Agent Bernard, or I'd be kicking the ladder out from beneath your ass."

Trevor chuckled. "I like a woman who knows to respect the evidence."

"Her father's a lycanthrope and a lawyer. Flirt at your own risk," Kenneth warned.

"If you're trying to mark your territory, come down here so I can laugh in your face." I shook my head. "Any idea how long she was dead before she was found hanging from the ceiling?"

"I won't be able to confirm anything until we've had a closer look at her, but judging from the setup, she was stiff when she was put up there and was just starting to soften when her body was discovered."

In ideal conditions, rigor mortis began four hours after death with eight hours being considered a typical average. That someone had stuffed her up there while she was stiff surprised me. "She'd be a lot harder to move during rigor mortis, and it's not a long window. Moving her probably sped the softening process, too."

I remembered his mention of the aversion lasting approximately an hour and a half, and I wondered how the killer's magic factored into the woman's time of death.

"Roughly. If she was outside, could be shorter, but from the looks of her, she'd been dead for around twelve hours before being found. I'm surprised. You actually know something about human decomposition."

"Call it an unhealthy interest in criminal law."

Kenneth sighed. "She's a lawyer, Trevor. She's also got this infuriating habit of understating her knowledge and abilities, so she might have enough schooling in forensics to make us look like slouches."

"Huh. Do you even have a suspect yet? A little early to be bringing in a lawyer."

"She's being recruited to be my partner. Apparently, my boss really wanted me on this case when I'm pretty certain Boulder has at least one office here and could've brought in someone local for this."

I sighed. "Your boss wants you out of narcotics and working with homicides."

"Not just homicides, serial killers." Kenneth sighed and climbed down. "It's a mess up there. What is that junk?"

"We're not sure, but we're looking at a few hours bagging everything."

"What a bloody mess. You have my cell?"

"The chief gave it to us."

"Give me a call if you find anything interesting. Let's go take a walk and see what we can find before they kill us for contaminating their crime scene."

"Want to see if we can find how the bodies were moved?"

"Exactly."

I nodded and followed his lead. Our first stop was to the lobby, where Kenneth ambushed the poor woman behind the desk and asked for a map of the resort. He dipped his hand into his pocket and pulled out a marker, uncapped it, and headed to the front doors. "We'll do the exterior first. If someone's using an aversion while we're doing this, we'll be able to see it on the map."

I frowned. "Really? Wouldn't we notice where we haven't checked?"

"No. It doesn't work like that unless it's a mutated ability. The aversion would make us completely forget about the place, so we wouldn't touch it on the map. Once the aversion wears off, it'll be the only place we haven't looked. If the aversion is really strong, it'll contaminate the map itself, so no one will notice we haven't been there until it wears off. It's a very dangerous ability, perfect for a killer who doesn't want to get caught."

"They could have all the time in the world with their victim and no one would go near them." I shuddered at the thought of being trapped with someone out to kill me with no hope of help. "Won't that make her dangerous to apprehend?"

"I'm armed, and being able to set an aversion doesn't make her immune to bullets. Stick close to me, and you should be fine. If we're separated and she gets you alone somewhere, no matter what happens, keep fighting."

"I will."

"Good. After we do our walk around, we'll go to our room. I'll teach you a few self-defense tricks that might help in a pinch."

"That might be a good idea."

Dad cleared his throat behind me, and I sighed. "If you say a single thing about what you'll do to him if I get a single bruise, we're joining forces and beating the sense back into you."

"You need to have your virus levels checked, Emma.

You're grouchy enough your mothers are worried about setting you off. You might murder your man before you have a chance to get laid. I tried telling them you'd probably be less grouchy after you get laid, but that earned me a double beating."

"Why haven't my mothers killed you yet?"

"They adore me. They'd miss me if they indulged in my murder. I also agreed to go with their harebrained scheme to try to marry you off so we can have another chick."

I eyed the nearest wall and wondered how hard I'd have to hit myself to make the pain go away. "Why hasn't it occurred to you idiots you can have another chick whenever you want? I'm an adult. I think I can handle my parents having another child. If you get rid of me, you lose your free babysitter."

"Your mothers made me swear to one at a time."

"My mothers are idiots."

"What are you two up to?"

"We're investigating," I replied, mindful of Kenneth's warning to keep investigative matters private.

"You're welcome to investigate with us. I'm concerned our jail bird may be one of the targets. So far, she fits the profile."

"I'd noticed a few disturbing similarities in the victims."

"You've seen them all?"

"Someone posted photographs of the bodies online, presented with a mention of the resort. They were taken after the bodies were found but before they were taken to the morgue. I'm willing to bet your killer's hanging around and wants everyone to know about the deaths." Dad grunted and ground his teeth together. "I hate when they're so damned proud of themselves. They want the notoriety. They want the attention."

"Or they want to send a message." Kenneth held up his new map of the resort. "We're going to get the lay of the land in case we've missed something or an aversion has been placed."

"There's been a lot of those around here, that's for sure." Dad fetched his phone and placed a call. "Hey, babe? Mind coming to take a walk around with the chicks? They want to do an evidence sweep and might get caught up in one of those aversions plaguing this place."

"Wait, what do you mean by plaguing the place?" I demanded.

"They've been popping up all over the resort all day. Guests have been complaining left and right it's taking a long time to get to their rooms. The elevators keep getting hit, which is making a mess of things."

I blinked, and it occurred to me we'd taken the stairs without thinking about it. "You're right. We took the stairs. Why the hell would we take the stairs from the top floor?"

"We needed the exercise."

I glared at Kenneth. "Maybe you need the exercise, but I'm in good shape, thank you. I dance every day."

"When are you going to dance today?"

"Before bed, if you must know."

"Can I watch?"

"Don't sound so hopeful. That's pathetic. I don't care if you watch, but it'll be boring for you."

"Emma, let the poor man flirt with you. He's trying to flirt with you. He's not doing a good job, but he's trying. You're going to have to be more aggressive than that, Agent Bernard. She's dense. That's from her ma's side of things."

Ma appeared, and as I didn't spot a flash of light, the evil wench of an angel had been spying on us while invisible again. "You're a bad person, Ma."

"Your father's right. If we don't give you a road map to follow, you'll get lost on the way, and I might never get any grandchicks."

"Ma, you're trying to get rid of me so you can have another baby."

"That, too. This way, everyone's happy. Have I applied enough pressure yet? I bribed him, and I'm not sure what I need to do to get you on the move. Where did I go wrong with you, Emma?"

"You didn't do anything wrong with her. She's perfect just like she is," Kenneth protested.

I shot him a look before glaring at Ma. "One of you is wrong, and I'm not sure who."

"If I told you, that'd ruin my fun," Ma replied.

"This is all your fault, Dad."

"Why is it my fault?"

"You couldn't pick a normal woman. No, you needed an angel, which meant you needed a succubus, and in a lapse of judgement, you picked my mothers. This is all your fault."

"I have no complaints with the situation." Dad laughed, shook his head, and herded me along. "One of these days you'll learn. The more you whine about it, the more we enjoy toying with you because we can. You should know this by now."

Kenneth looked me in the eyes and said, "How have you not killed them yet?"

"I really don't know."

BLOODSTAINS MARKED where the third woman's body had been found, and had the serial killer put her in the dumpster rather than behind it, it would've taken a long time for someone to find her. A body buried in the bottom of a full dumpster might make it to the local dump or junkyard, effectively ensuring a difficult—or impossible—investigation. The bloodstains worried me; the other victims hadn't bled much, most of the fluids a consequence of decomposition rather than physical violence.

Bloodstains pointed at a different cause of death, be it a from a shooting or stabbing. While bloodied noses could leave stains, the volume pointed at a lethal injury.

It also pointed at a murder of opportunity, one that'd taken place on site rather.

"That's a curious expression," Kenneth announced, nudging me with his elbow. "What's on your mind?"

"The other murders had the victim relocated. With this much blood, do you think she was moved after death?"

Dad grunted, crouching by the bloodstains, and he shook his head. "As far as we can tell, she was killed here. An aversion kept anyone from finding her until late last night. That's our current theory."

"Time of death?" Kenneth asked.

"From what I can tell from the photographs I saw, I'd bet early morning yesterday before the dance retreat started."

We had a busy serial killer on our hands—or killers. Several people working together could make the timing work, although the pulley system led me to believe someone weak, likely a woman, held sole responsibility for the deaths. "Brown hair, blue eyes, my build?"

"Of the three victims, this woman looks closest to you," my father replied.

Shit. I ran my fingers through my hair and gave my scalp a good scratch. "All right. Do you have a copy of the picture, Dad?"

"I do." He retrieved his phone, unlocked it, and tossed it to me. "I saved the entire lot to my pictures."

Whoever she was, the killer enjoyed taking pictures of her victims, which offered a wealth of information about their deaths. The third victim did resemble me, and the killer had stabbed her more times than I cared to count. I compared the image with the bloodstains, narrowing my eyes. "I think she was moved." I held the phone to Kenneth. "That's not nearly enough blood for the number of stab wounds in that photo."

Kenneth took my father's phone and sighed. "I bet the body bag's in the dumpster."

"We're going to have to go dumpster diving, won't we?"

"We are."

I considered the options and fixated on the worst-case scenario. "And because it's our investigation, we get to do it, don't we?"

"It's like you've done this before. I hope you're not too attached to your clothes. Let's grab a box of gloves and get to work."

"Because gloves are going to save us from a dumpster?"

"No, so we don't leave our fingerprints on anything we pull out of the dumpster. The forensics guys should have bags we can use to sort through the trash."

"Think they have some clothes pins?"

"Why?"

I pinched my nose closed with my fingers and pointed at the dumpster with my other hand. As I didn't want to sound like a duck, I arched a brow and waited for him to figure out what I meant.

"Won't hurt to ask." Kenneth sighed and headed for the hotel. I followed, regretting my choice to attend the retreat. We returned to the crew still working at clearing out the ceiling. "Got a spare box of gloves and bags? We need to go through the dumpster."

One of the two men hard at work tossed the requested items down and managed to smack Kenneth in the head with both.

"Nice aim," I complimented, bending over to grab the gloves and leaving the bags for Kenneth. I glanced at my father and smiled. "Guess who gets to help with the dumpster diving? My parents. Aren't you so happy you conned me into helping the FBI today?" To make it clear I wasn't accepting no for an answer, I handed the box of gloves to Dad. "And no magic tricks from either of my mothers."

"You're feeling vindictive today."

"You got a room at this hotel through nefarious means."

"A cancellation isn't nefarious, Emma."

"It is now."

Kenneth shook his head, caught my elbow, and pulled me down the hall. "However entertaining it is to watch you argue with your father, we have a dumpster to search."

Someone from the ceiling tossed another box of smaller bags down along with a marker, which my father retrieved. "Don't mess up any evidence."

"He's talking to you," Kenneth informed me.

I stepped on his foot. "No, he's not. He's probably talking to my father."

"I'm talking to all of you!" the forensics guy howled.

I scowled while Kenneth laughed. "It's not funny."

"It is funny. Give it a few months. You'll laugh whenever you can. The rest of the time? You'll be wishing you hadn't gotten out of bed in the morning."

I turned my glare to my father. "Is this really what you want for your only child? A life of wishing I hadn't gotten out of bed in the morning?"

"Don't be a drama queen, Emma. It's not that bad."

DANCING skills and superb balance didn't make me immune to leaning too far forward straining to reach the next damned piece of refuse for sorting. With an indignant squawk, I tumbled head first into the dumpster, landing with a crunch, a crash, and a squish.

Without the squish, I might've endured without screaming, but a wet, sticky, oozing substance accompanied the squish, which my nose immediately recognized as decaying organic matter, likely of human origin.

I'd never forget the stench of human decay.

I launched out of the dumpster, landed in a crouch beside the dumpster, and fought the urge to run screaming to the nearest bathroom. "I found a body," I announced.

Huh. Who knew I could sound almost calm following screaming my head off and flying out of a dumpster without the benefit of wings?

Kenneth rubbed his forehead, grabbed his phone, and called someone. "I need a team to the dumpster behind the resort. It appears we might have another body. We're also going to need a change of clothes for my partner, as hers will need to be confiscated for evidence collection. Bring in a woman for the base examination, please." Kenneth pulled his phone away from his ear. "Will you need an ambulance, Emma?"

"No. I need a change of clothes and a head to toe decontamination."

My father sighed. "I'll go to your room and bring the clothes if you give me the key."

"Take mine," Kenneth ordered, pulling out his wallet. "No ambulance, just sanitizer safe for lycanthropes. Thanks."

My father took the room key from Kenneth and herded my mothers to the room.

"If you even think about doing anything inappropriate in Kenneth's suite, I'll add three bodies to the dumpster," I warned.

The trio dared to laugh at me.

Kenneth stood on his toes and peered into the dumpster. "You did find a body. Looks like you dislodged the garbage hiding her when you fell in."

"Brown hair?"

"Yep."

If I ever got my hands on the serial killer, there'd be another murder: hers. How brutal the murder would be depended on a lot of factors, including what weapons I had at my disposal and if I could figure out how to use them.

The instant I made it home, I'd accept Kenneth's offer of self-defense lessons, and I'd one-up him with the inclusion of creative fighting lessons. Surely I could find someone who could teach me how to use anything handy to protect myself.

I wouldn't tell my instructor I had secondary motivations involving the brutal murders of serial killers with a fetish for women with brown hair.

"Today is the worst, Kenneth."

"I know. I'm sorry. I'll make it up to you somehow."

"Fortunately for you, this isn't your fault."

"Do I want to know what you'd do if it were my fault?"

"You'd be joining her in the dumpster. It's up for debate if you'd be breathing when you joined her."

"I've met a lot of lycanthropes, but you're one of the crankiest."

Kenneth's amusement annoyed me, but I settled with wrinkling my nose at him. "What's the plan now?"

"Once the team gets here, you'll be checked head to toe for evidence, your clothing will be confiscated, and the technician will give you a basic medical check over to ensure you're fine and don't need to be treated for shock. Fairly standard protocol. It won't take too long, and the tech will probably do it in a bathroom so you won't put on a show for the entire resort."

"Small blessings."

"Hey, at least you won't have to do this in an ambulance. That's common."

"I'm very grateful a bathroom is an option."

"All that said, I'm really impressed you didn't puke. I might have." Kenneth peeked into the dumpster again. "Scratch that. I definitely would have."

"I screamed. That's almost as bad."

"Don't sweat it, Emma. I probably would've screamed, too."

"Well, that's something at least."

TEN

Assuming I lived long enough, I'd be
able to fly one day.

Plans often led to disappointment, and I questioned why I bothered making them. If I lived life off the cuff, I wouldn't have to deal with my plans falling apart. No matter how hard I thought about it, I couldn't remember how I'd become separated from Kenneth, the forensics lady responsible for collecting my clothes and checking for evidence, or my parents.

How the hell had I gotten into a basement worthy of a horror movie? Add some graffiti, and a movie studio wouldn't need to do any editing for atmosphere.

I blamed magic. Magic could alter memories, coerce people into doing things against their will, and create more problems than I cared to think about. Most had some special trick, but I'd never tried to find mine. Having Dad's lycanthropy virus had been enough for me.

Assuming I lived long enough, I'd be able to fly one day.

Unless I figured out what was going on and why, I

wouldn't be flying anywhere. I worried I'd end up as corpse number five.

I should've asked Kenneth to stop, drop, and teach me something about self-defense before we'd walked anywhere. Then again, wandering around the resort with the forensics lady, my parents, or Kenneth should've been as safe as it got.

A soft laugh behind me sent chills creeping through me. I turned and came face to face with Cathy.

"You just can't seem to help yourself, can you? You have to take as many men as possible, don't you?"

Stupidity needed to be criminalized. "What are you talking about?"

"Kenneth wasn't enough for you, so you had to take that other hunk, too?"

Other hunk? What other hunk? I blinked, and it struck me there was only one other man I'd been keeping company with at the resort: Dad. "Uh, about this tall, brown hair, a bit too muscular for his own good, dressed in jeans and a dress shirt?"

"Yes, him."

"That's my father."

Cathy gaped. "What?"

"He's my father. You saw the angel, I presume?"

"Yes. I'd been wondering about that."

In a way, I was relieved; her reply confirmed I hadn't hallucinated walking with Kenneth and my parents. I could handle a memory lapse, which I presumed was some form of compulsion meant to lure me to her. If she layered an aversion targeting Ma, Dad, Kenneth, and the forensics lady before compelling me to follow her, I could understand how we'd been separated.

It also meant the woman was a lot more dangerous than I'd thought.

As appeasing her curiosity might help me live longer, I opted for the route of cooperation. The only way to lie to an angel was through omission, and I'd done it enough times to Ma I held hope I could trick the other dancer for a while. "She's one of my mothers. Dad wanted to talk to Agent Bernard, so I was walking with them."

"He's mine."

I needed to have a long talk with Kenneth about how much trouble he made for me whenever he breathed the same air I did. Worse, I'd have to lecture him about his unforgivable tendency to make me like sharing space with him.

I hadn't even had a chance to put much thought into if I wanted to give him a chance to contract my virus. I figured I'd get there eventually, assuming the psychotic drug dealer didn't kill me first. "That's between you two. It's not any of my business."

Yet. It wasn't any of my business yet, and as soon as I decided either way if I'd accept any moves from him, once it was my business, Cathy would regret her decision to lure me off.

I had nails and teeth. I could do some damage to the bitch's pretty face.

Damn it, Dad was right. I needed to have my virus levels checked again. Violence wasn't supposed to be my first solution to problems, especially when I couldn't fight my way out of a wet cardboard box.

"Are you sure?"

"I'm a fond supporter of free will, Cathy." I was also fond of living, and I didn't want to find out through personal experience if she was the person killing dancers with too close of a resemblance to me. "I came here to dance."

"You seemed pretty disappointed when Kenneth called your name."

"There's a reason for that." It involved my tested patience and my lycanthropy virus, two things she didn't need to know. "I came here to expand my skills for work."

"For work? You? You don't look like a professional."

"I work at a theater as an on-call replacement if a dancer is out and is mandatory for a performance. I learn the routines of the important roles as a backup in case of emergency. When I'm not doing that, I handle the other backup dancers and work backstage."

"You're really a professional."

I shrugged. "I'll never be a prima ballerina, but I like the work. Most of the time, I'm just a nameless face on the stage filling in so the show can go on. The theater is undergoing renovations right now, so it was perfect timing to go to the retreat."

While pretending to pay close attention to Cathy, I checked out the basement for routes of escape. The wasted space annoyed me. Why have such a large basement and not use it? Surely a resort needed storage space.

A thought crossed my mind, one I didn't like at all. What if I wasn't at the resort anymore? The building could easily be part of a windowless warehouse somewhere.

"This isn't what I expected. Getting the amateurs out of the way is one thing, but career dancers? No, the world needs more of the serious dancers around. What am I going to do with you? This wasn't part of my plans!"

I'd been lured into the clutches of a psychopath, and like every other serial killer I'd read about in college, she had a skewed view on life, an agenda, and a purpose, which made her dangerous. "What were your plans?"

If I got lucky, she'd view it as an invitation to spill all her secrets. I wondered if I could land a spot as the prosecuting lawyer. I could take Colorado's bar exam and pass it with a little work. I bet Dad wouldn't mind spotting me for a long-term hotel in exchange for me kicking the bitch's ass in court.

I just needed proof she'd been behind the murders.

"I only want Kenneth. Once he's mine, I have no plans. A few kids, I guess. We'll make beautiful babies."

Passion so often dictated a person's course of action destroying and creating life in equal measure. How many lives would Cathy destroy before she got what she wanted?

"I guess those other women had infringed on your turf?"

"They're his type, and I can't have any competition. He's always appreciated a challenge. He'll appreciate the unsolvable mystery I've left for him."

"Unsolvable? Unsolvable how?"

Cathy waved her hand. "Oh, it's simple. My magic ensures they can't check any of the sites thoroughly. They'll never figure it out. I took my time with them and made sure to protect the important evidence, of course. His colleagues like to think they're so smart."

While we hadn't pieced together Cathy was the one behind the bodies, we'd already narrowed the suspect pool to a woman without much effort. "Oh. That's clever."

Not.

"I know, right? Do you want to see how I did it? You're not a threat. Hell, you don't even like him. This'll work. I can help you with your career, you can help me. It's perfect."

Mental illness could happen to anyone, but I'd never met

someone so obviously afflicted I didn't need a professional to diagnose that Cathy had entered batshit crazy territory. "You want me to help you?"

Manic glee lit her expression, and she grabbed my hand, pulling me across the open space towards one of the doors. "It's perfect. This one's too heavy for me to carry on my own, although I haven't finished with her yet. It took me weeks to ensure she'd come here so I could get her alone. You can help me finish her off. I'm taking the slow route with her. She's gotten close to my Kenneth one too many times. It'll take a few more hours before I'm ready for the next stage. We'll have to wait a while before we move her. She'll be easier to drag around after she starts stiffening up."

I wouldn't blame Dad's contribution of the lycanthropy virus for my desire to beat Cathy into a vaguely human-shaped puddle. "I see. Where is she?"

I'd start the beating as soon as I could and try to help her next victim. I could only hope I wouldn't be too late.

CATHY GUIDED me through a door which led into a small room lit with battery-powered lanterns in the corners. Someone had knocked out the concrete wall to access the raw earth and stone behind it before digging a tunnel large enough we could walk through without touching the ceiling. Ruts in the loose soil exposed where she had dragged a cart or wheelbarrow down the passage countless times.

"Watch your step. The last one threw up on the floor. Wouldn't want you to step in it."

Gross. I followed in her footsteps, my gaze locked on her throat. I understand the desire to strangle someone; the thought of wrapping my hands around Cathy's throat tempted me far too much.

I'd have a hard case, but I could get away with a justifiable homicide charge. If I saw her victim, I'd be able to get away with manslaughter in defense of another along with a self-defense acquittal if I played my cards right. I bet Dad would be happy to defend me despite the case not falling under his typical narcotics defense umbrella.

The tunnel opened up to a small, dug-out room primed for collapse, illuminated with more camping lanterns. Without any visible support structures and a lot of loosely packed soil making up the walls, it was only a matter of time before it fell in on itself. A hose dangled from a hole in the ceiling with a nozzle attached to the end, the handle taped so it showered water into a pit below. I bet the moisture would elevate the collapse risk given time.

Or flood the whole place out.

I really didn't need more problems.

Cathy pointed at the center of the room. "She's in there. I gagged her because I got tired of listening to her screaming."

I took a few tentative steps forward, keeping an eye on the lunatic masterminding the murders of other dancers, and peeked over the edge. Sure enough, a gagged and bound woman sat at the bottom of the pit, which slowly filled with water.

I eased away from the hole so I wouldn't join her. "Interesting."

"Isn't it?" Cathy hopped forward a step to admire her handiwork.

I wound up and punched the bitch in the throat. When that didn't do more than make her gasp and choke out a cry, I did it again, putting more force behind the blow.

Four hits later, she collapsed to her knees, clutching at her neck.

"You're a piece of shit." I spotted a worn, mud-encrusted shovel leaning against the wall, snatched it, and to make sure she stayed down, I swung with every bit of my strength and smashed it over her head.

Cathy slumped into a heap at my feet.

Later, I might even feel guilty for sucker punching the woman, but I had bigger things to worry about. I had no idea how long the woman had been in the pit, and if it filled up with too much water, she'd drown. I dropped my improvised weapon, headed for the hose, and grabbed it, going to work unraveling the rope so I could shut the damned thing off. Tired of fighting with the layers of duct tape, I kinked the hose, tied it in a knot to make sure it stayed kinked, and scowled that I'd only managed to reduce the flow.

In the future, I'd start carrying a pocketknife everywhere I went. By the time I finished picking off the tape enough I could stop the water, my fingers ached, I was soaked, and I wanted to whip Cathy with it for being a pain in the ass. I didn't even know if the woman below was still alive.

I approached the hole, eyed the distance down, and wondered if I'd be able to climb up once I got down there. With the shovel, I could probably manage something. Sighing, I retrieved the probable murder weapon, cursed myself for being my ma's daughter, and slid over the edge and splashed down beside Cathy's victim.

My first move was to remove the gag, a long strip of duct tape, with a single, hard yank.

I didn't blame the woman for screaming. "Sorry."

"That fucking hurt!"

I always loved when introductions turned sour from the

get go, though there wasn't much I could do about the situation. "Sorry. It would've hurt more if I tried to pick it off. Fast, brutal, but over."

"You're not her."

"No, I'm not. She lured me here." I crouched beside her, kneeling in the water, and eyeing the woman's wrists, which were bound with duct tape. Cursing Cathy, I went to work setting the woman free. "I'm Emma."

"Emma? Emma Sansaul?"

I froze. "You know my name?"

"Oh. This is not good. This is not good at all."

Puzzled, I resumed my work setting her free, having doubts about the entire situation. "Why is this not good?"

"Isn't your father some hot shot attorney?"

"Well, he certainly thinks so." Damned egotistical, aggressive swan. "Not sure how that's relevant to this situation, though."

"That woman's up for a drug trial and wants him representing her so she can clear her name. If she gets a hold of you, she can get what she wants."

"Well, that's the dumbest fucking thing I've ever heard in my life."

"What? Why would you say that? It's true!"

I shook my head, jerking at the tape to get it to separate. The water didn't help, making it hard to get a good hold of the slippery material. "Ma's an angel, Mom's a succubus, and Dad's a lycanthrope. I'd call her pretty dumb to go toe-to-toe with that trio. Cathy's a real chatter, isn't she?"

"She likes to gloat. We need to hurry before she comes back."

"I punched her in the throat and smashed her over the head with her own shovel. If she gets up from that anytime soon, I'll be surprised. I'm more worried about this damned place collapsing in on itself."

"You smashed her over the head with a shovel?"

"Easy acquittal. I could run the case with my eyes closed. Self-defense and in defense of another stacked together makes for a pretty strong case in my favor. They'll toss the charges, especially since she's been classified as a serial killer."

"She has been? How do you know?"

"Some idiot thought it would be a good idea to have me help find her, that's how I know."

"You're serious. You're in the FBI? I thought you were a dancer."

"I am a dancer. I just happen to also be a lawyer, and for some reason, this translates to being FBI material. In good news, I'm not in the FBI yet. I'm just a tag along. Honestly, I think it's pretty ridiculous."

"I'm Jolene. Jolene Bernard."

I groaned, bowed my head, and sighed. "You're related to Kenneth, aren't you?"

"Wait. You know Kenneth? He's my brother. That's why I'm here. That bitch didn't like that I spent so much time with him. She didn't believe me when I tried to tell her he's my brother."

Maybe I could dodge the whole part about knowing Kenneth, the probability of being stuck with him for life, and my mixed emotions on the subject. Would he even want me around after he found out I'd surprise attacked someone, punched her in the throat, and beat her with a shovel?

"How'd you end up here?" After a few more yanks, I freed Jolene's hands and dropped the tape into the water. "Sorry if that hurt."

"Beats being tied up down here, so don't worry about it. Anyway, I was tailing my brother. He wouldn't tell me why he was going to Boulder, so I followed him here. Well, I arrived two days before he was supposed to and told the family I was going on a work trip. Before I had a chance to find him, she grabbed me, tied me up, and dumped me in this hole."

"Well, I can help with getting you out of this hole, but you'll have to deal with your brother problems on your own."

She snorted. "As always. Why does he always find the damned lunatics?"

"Wait, what?"

"I bet he came here looking for some lunatic druggie he fell for during a bust. I tried to tell him to avoid the low-life druggies, but no."

I sat in the water, lowered my head, and ran my fingers through my hair. "He said something about a jail bird, didn't he?"

"You do know Kenneth. Yes, he did. The whole family is worried about it. He's obviously smitten, and it's not like him to mix work with his personal life like that."

At somewhere around two feet deep, if I flopped over and took a nap, I'd inevitably drown, which had some advantages in the grand scheme of things. "If I told you that it was a huge misunderstanding, would you believe me?"

"No, not when it comes to my brother!"

"I probably wouldn't, either. If I had a brother or sister. Had to try."

"What are you talking about?"

"Would you consider anyone who uses pixie dust a low-life druggie?"

"Well, no. Not at all. It's legal. Unless you get the higher grades, and honestly, who hasn't wanted a hit of that stuff?"

"Well, my mother thought it would be funny to get me drunk and give me a stash of the highest-grade stuff, resulting in an eventful evening at a bar."

Jolene stared at me, her mouth dropping open while she blinked.

I waited for her to work through the reality of my announcement.

"You're his jail bird?"

"A single night in solitary because I really shouldn't ever get a hold of the good pixie dust. It took three rounds of neutralizer to counter. They let me out when I had two functioning brain cells and adult supervision. An angel verified I had no idea what grade the dust was, so I wasn't charged with anything. Dad would've loved that case had it made it through the courts."

Jolene snickered, sucked in a breath, and hiccupped. "This explains so much. You're his type, and you have a ridiculous bar bust story. No wonder his engine got revved. I'm sorry. I had no idea it was something like that. I thought you were..."

"Like Chatty Cathy the Serial Killer up there?"

"Yeah, like her."

I'd probably go to hell, but I'd enjoy the trip. "We should get out of this pit and hit her with the shovel again. She's killed at least four people over him."

"She what?"

"She murdered four people."

"But why?"

"I'm going with psychotic, mentally ill, obsessed with your brother, and jealous."

"My brother's not going to like that at all."

"He's also been transferred out of narcotics to serial killers because of this. The FBI might have a few loose bolts in management as someone thought it was a good idea."

"Oh, shit. They've put him back on homicides? He's going to be a bear about that. He hates working with a partner."

I would let Kenneth break that news to her, assuming I didn't run away at the first opportunity and become a hermit. After the day I had, the idea tempted me. "Serial killers, specifically."

"How do you even know this?"

"Well, that's where things get a little complicated."

"You mean they weren't already?"

While she had a good point, I shrugged, scrambled back to my feet, and grabbed the shovel, eyeing the wall and digging a few foot holds so we could scramble out. "Well, it started when I almost missed my flight. I boarded at the last minute to discover the only open seat was next to your brother."

"Oh, dear. Was he a pest?"

"When isn't he a pest?" I complained, pointing at my fresh holes. "You go first. I'll boost you up if you need it."

"All right." Without any help from me, Jolene climbed out of the pit. I handed the shovel up for her before joining her.

Cathy hadn't moved from where I'd left her, and before I could stop her, Jolene grabbed the shovel, lifted it over her head, and cracked the business end into Cathy's skull. Twice.

"Well, if she wasn't dead before, she probably is now."

Jolene scowled, eyed the woman, and hit her a few extra times. "How badly do you think I've screwed up my chances to claim self-defense?"

"If my first hit killed her, I think you'll get off with potential mutilation of a corpse, and with a little work, I expect the charges would be dropped. Circumstances would be considered, and being dumped in a hole and slowly drowned will probably earn you the sympathy of the jury."

"How about you?"

"The jury likes heroics, rescue stories, and the like. Self-defense is an easy one for me, especially when I include how you were being slowly drowned. I think we'll be fine."

"Huh. Who knew lawyers could be useful to have around? Maybe we shouldn't have killed her. Yet, that is. Killed her yet. I'm pretty sure the bitch deserved to die."

Maybe I needed to have my virus levels checked, but Jolene looked ready to start gnawing on Cathy's body. "That would have become a premeditated murder charge, and those are a lot harder to dodge, Jolene."

"You're probably right."

I stared at the body at our feet and shook my head at the insanity of it all.

ELEVEN

JOLENE WANTED to dump Cathy's body in the hole, cover her, and leave without anyone ever knowing she'd been held captive by a serial killer. I understood the stung pride side of things. I had a gap in my memories, and the instant I called my parents, I'd have a lot of explaining to do and no way to satisfy them.

Unfortunately for us, our phones were gone, which meant we had to use Cathy's, which would screw with evidence and leave our prints on her shit, but I figured an emergency counted as a good reason to mess around with the crime scene.

It wasn't like I had any choice in the matter. Bracing myself for the worst, I dialed Ma's number, grateful I had a single bar of reception.

Jolene played with the shovel and Cathy's head, and I turned away so I wouldn't have to watch the woman finish mutilating the body.

"I see you found a phone," Ma answered. "It's not yours."

"I killed someone, and I'm using her phone to tell you about it." The fastest way to get Ma on the move was to hang up on her, so I did, and I waited.

Even expecting Ma to show up, the flash of golden light startled me so much I jumped, tripped over my own feet, and plunged into the hole. I landed hard, swallowed water, and choked on it.

The terror of drowning in a death pit made by a psychotic serial killer surged through me, and the next thing I knew, feathers burst in a cloud around me and I honked my alarm.

Fuck.

Ma leaned over the edge. "It seems your father was right. You really do need to get your virus levels checked."

The lycanthropy virus did a lot of things, but it didn't teach me how to be a swan, and it took me an embarrassingly long time to figure out how to swim without feeling like I was about to roll over and breathe water again.

"You're not going to drown, Emma. Settle down. You don't even need to work hard to float. Just let it happen. You could rest your head on your back and take a nap without having to worry about a thing."

Jolene joined Ma and gaped at me. "You're a lycanthrope?"

"She sure is. And it's her first shift, too. She's been hissing mad for days, and frankly, I'm surprised her father didn't take her to the CDC to have her virus levels checked before she came here. Really, Emma. If you can't cool your temper, you can stay down there for a while. You're worse than George sometimes."

"George?"

"Her father, of course. You look like you've had a rough day, missy."

"Jolene."

"Agent Bernard's little sister, yes. Your mother called him and told him you'd disappeared. We found out not long after Emma wandered off."

"Lured, like me. That bitch did it."

"Well, she won't be doing it again, that's for sure. Was tenderizing the body necessary?"

"Yes. She had me in that hole and was going to drown me."

"Yes, I can understand why you'd want to beat her with a muddy shovel. A forgivable enough sin, I suppose. She was already dead."

"I can live with a count of mutilation of a body."

"I see Emma already informed you of the potential crimes involved. Just like her." One day, I'd figure out how an angel sighed. One day. I'd have to stalk Ma and do some intensive studying.

Ma sighed again. "No, Emma. You do not. Think quieter so I can call your father."

I tested Ma's claim I could bury my beak in my feathers on my back and float without drowning. It worked well enough I only hissed my irritation at being stuck in the pit with no idea how to get out on my own.

"George, I seem to have startled our little chick into her first shift, and she fell in a hole." Ma leaned over the pit's edge again. "She's about as big as you are, and she's currently hissing because she has no idea how to get out of the hole she fell into. Maybe if you weren't so flighty, Emma, you wouldn't be stuck in a hole right now. Be a dear and tell Agent Bernard

Emma located his sister. She's fine, although I'm afraid she's guilty of a count of body mutilation. Emma took offense to being lured away from us and used a shovel with lethal force. Clearly self-defense. Miss Bernard took out some of her temper on the body after being freed. As for location, we're on the outskirts of Boulder beneath an abandoned warehouse. I'm cheating a little to get better reception. Do bring some dry clothes for the girls when you come. You may want to give Agent Bernard the complete disclosure of what to expect from a cranky first-shift lycanthrope. No, George. She's cranky. She's been hissing non-stop since I called you. I'll leave the phone in the warehouse above for you so you can track it." Ma hung up, and her phone vanished. "There. Your father will handle the details. Agent Bernard is quite miffed you gave us the slip. I thought you'd appreciate the warning."

Jolene snorted. "Wasn't her fault. That bitch had tricky magic. From what I gathered, she can take over someone once, and that's how she gets them where she wants them to go, and she uses that repulsion magic of hers to make sure no one notices it happening."

"That's how she caught you."

"Right."

"Well, she won't be doing that again. She's quite dead."

"Good."

"Now we just need to settle in to wait for the cavalry to arrive. Why don't you tell me everything that happened from the beginning? I think you'll find questioning will go much smoother with an angel on your side."

MA KEPT Jolene company while I floated in a pit and got my white feathers muddy. The few times I'd tried to put my wings to good use, I'd collided with the wall, and no amount of honking or hissing enlightened me about how to fly or escape without help.

"Jolene, are you all right?" Kenneth demanded.

I tried to bury my entire head in my feathers, ultimately forced to hide under my own wing to escape the embarrassment.

"I'm fine."

"You don't look fine."

"I'm muddy. That's it. And you might have to arrest me, apparently?"

"Typically, we don't arrest victims of kidnapping and attempted murder for using force to escape their situation."

"A count of body mutilation."

"I'm going to pretend you didn't tell me that. It's like you want me to arrest you."

"I'm just being honest."

"Be honest when you're not covered in mud and weren't in line to be victim number five of a serial killer!" Kenneth howled.

"That's not my fault."

Dad crouched at the edge of the pit and stared at me, a brow arched. "You're absolutely filthy. What have you been doing down there? Rolling in it?"

"She tried to climb out a few times and learned the hard way she doesn't have enough room to take flight. I was hoping she'd figure out how to shift back on her own, but I've determined I was being unreasonable."

"It's better for her to stay a swan for at least a few more

hours. It'll give her virus a chance to recover from her shift," Dad replied. "You all right down there?"

I lifted my head, drew in as deep a breath as I could, and protested my situation in a honk.

"Well, I'm going to go out on a limb and say your lungs are healthy." Dad took off his shirt and tossed it to someone, and his pants followed a moment later, leaving him in a pair of boxers. He jumped in beside me, grabbed hold of my neck, and held me in place while he looked me over. I hissed and honked, struggling to pull free of his grip.

"Stop your whining. I'm not hurting you. I'm making sure all your pieces are situated in the appropriate fashion. They are, in case you were wondering. Good conformation, all your feathers seem intact, although you're not going to like getting all that mud out. We'll have to soap you off and possibly apply oil to your feathers, although shifting usually fixes any soap-induced damage. Be grateful for that."

I bet Dad held my neck so I couldn't bite him, and I hissed my displeasure at being thwarted.

"She wants to bite you, George," Ma announced.

"I guessed as much. Kenneth? Do you really want her? She's going to be a handful for the next few weeks, and you will emerge with a few scars, possibly some broken bones, and damage to your pride and ego."

"What's going on?" Jolene asked. "Why is he asking you that, Ken?"

I foresaw a few uncomfortable minutes while Kenneth explained the situation.

"The angel bribed me to marry her daughter, and I'm trying to figure out how to get Emma to agree to it. I under-estimated how much lycanthropes can eat, though. I'm going to have to renegotiate the terms with this new information."

"Done," Ma said. "I'll add an appropriate amount to ensure she's properly fed."

I honked a protest over Ma trying to sell me to Kenneth again.

"I'm not selling you, silly chick. I'm bribing him to pursue you. There's a difference."

"Ken?" Jolene demanded.

"What? I'm not going to deny it. Do you know how many dance theaters I went to trying to figure out where she worked so I could watch her perform? I worked overtime to pay for all those tickets."

Silence fell over us, and Dad broke it with a rumbling chuckle. "Why didn't you just ask me in court, Kenneth? I would've told you where she worked."

"I didn't realize she was your daughter," he replied, his tone sheepish. "I knew you had the same last name, but since the case wasn't going to court, I didn't have any access to other information, and I didn't look closely at her identification during the arrest. Had I, I would've abused my powers and run her address."

Dad snickered, and I clacked my beak and hissed at him. "That would've saved you some trouble."

"You're making her want to bite you again, George," Ma announced.

Mom laughed and leaned over, and to make it clear I was a freak of nature, she'd showed up in her natural form, and mocked me with a sensuous stretch of her back wings.

Bitch.

Ma laughed. "I'm not going to repeat what she's thinking about you."

"It's not every day I get to show off without her getting an attitude about it. Clamp her beak closed so we don't have to listen to her making a fuss."

"No. She's cranky enough without adding to it. All right, little chick. I'm going to toss you up there. Try not to hurt yourself attacking either one of your mothers. Let's try to get through your first shift without a maiming."

Without waiting for my approval, Dad worked an arm under me, picked me up, and launched me into the air. I honked my alarm, spread my wings, and flapped. I stayed aloft for a few seconds before crashing into the dirt at Kenneth's feet.

I rolled to my feet, reared back, and spread my wings, opening my beak and eyeing potential targets. Who would I bite first?

All three of my parents deserved a hard nip.

Kenneth chuckled, seized my neck beneath my head, and wrapped his arm around my chest, pulling me towards him. "Easy, jail bird. A bath, a good dinner, a change of clothes, and some time to dance your heart out will help, and you don't need to beat your parents today. We said we'd negotiate on that tomorrow."

I hissed, straining to reach Dad, who climbed out of the hole covered in mud.

"You figured out the magic combination to appease the beast," my father observed.

"She's not hard to understand. Everything that delayed her from dancing upset her, so she needs a chance to get some dancing in because dancing is probably how she relaxes and copes with the unexpected. Lycanthropes eat a lot, although her card made it look like she wasn't anywhere near her first shift. I've seen some of my co-workers eat, and they can clean out a grocery store if they've had to shift a lot in one day. As for the bath, that one's obvious. You need one just as bad as she does, Mr. Sansaul."

"I noticed." Dad grabbed the hose and washed off the worst of the mud before pulling on his jeans. "Wrap her in my shirt. I don't want to force water into her feathers and get her cold. We're resistant to illness, but we can get sick just like regular humans."

Ma took Dad's shirt and approached. "Put your wings down, young lady. We're going to clear out and let the police handle the situation from here. They should be arriving within the next few minutes. Miss Bernard, I trust you'll make yourself accessible for questioning?"

"Of course."

"Excellent."

As Ma would abuse her angelic powers to make me do what she wanted, I lowered my wings and limited my protests to silent promises of payback at a later date, which made her laugh. She used Dad's shirt to towel me off, and once satisfied, she stole Dad's jacket and wrapped it around me. "Think you can handle seventy or so pounds of angry swan, Kenneth?"

"Unless she wants me carrying her, she can walk. If she does want me to carry her, I'll figure something out."

I waddled towards the tunnel to make it clear I had no interest in being carried.

TWELVE

A little soap isn't going to hurt her.

CLEANING A SWAN INVOLVED FOUR PEOPLE, one jet tub, dish soap Dad declared safe for waterfowl, and so much cursing Ma refused to stay in the room. I thought I handled it well. I didn't bite anyone, and I limited my protests to the occasional hiss. Kenneth handled most of the work, soaping my feathers and rinsing out the suds until he was satisfied.

If he'd listened to Dad, we would've been finished a lot faster.

"A little soap isn't going to hurt her," my father promised. "This can go one of two ways. Once I help her shift back to human, she might be energized, or she might collapse and need to sleep it off. Either way, we need to call in a CDC rep to check her virus levels; she was tested three months ago, and her levels were nowhere near what is needed for a first shift."

Kenneth got to his feet, dried his hands, and fetched his phone. "I'll take care of the rep and check in with Chief

Rochester to see what we're going to need to do about the murders."

"You're probably going to be done with this case within a day; you're going to have to disclose you're connected to someone involved, which will bump another pair onto the case, not that there's much of one."

"That woman was a lunatic," Jolene muttered, watching from the bathroom door. "Who the hell was she, Ken?"

"Her name's Cathy Poulette, a drug addict and dealer I busted a few years ago."

"That explains it, especially since you were hitting all the theaters. She tracked you?"

"She must have. I didn't exactly hide I was looking for a dancer, and I wasn't having any luck with internet searches. For a professional, you're hard to find, jail bird."

"She stands in for sick or injured dancers. It's not exactly a prestigious job," Dad replied. "And don't get me wrong. I'm very proud of my daughter, but she's always been happier making sure things don't fall apart than taking the spotlight. Her work hit the right balance with her. She got to dance a lot, as she had to learn the routines, but she could avoid the stress of moving a lot and the general disadvantages of performance. There was a lot of pressure on her, but she liked the challenge her work provided."

"I think she'd prefer to speak for herself. Has she been a swan long enough to safely shift?"

Dad nodded and shooed everyone else out of the bathroom. "I'll bring her out in a few minutes, so you just wait in the other room. I expect she'll be napping within a few minutes."

"I'll make sure her bed's ready," Kenneth replied, darting out of the room.

Mom rolled her eyes, flung her hands in the air, and followed. Jolene stared at me for a long moment, shrugged, and closed the bathroom door behind her.

"All right, Emma. This'll take some getting used to, but try to think about the thing that makes you a human more than anything else. Focus on it and reclaim it. Your virus isn't your enemy, and the faster you accept both sides of you, the faster and easier it'll be for you to shift. Your virus will always have a mind of its own, but it's a lot easier to control when you're not fighting it all the time." Dad stroked his hand over my head and ruffled my feathers. "Go on and give it a shot."

What made me human? What made anyone human?

I didn't even have a chance to think it through before pain ripped through me. I shifted, and instead of making friends with my virus, I made acquaintances with the floor.

THE MURMUR of conversation woke me, and I cracked open an eye to discover the door to the living room of the suite cracked open. Mom slipped into my bedroom, grinned, and closed the door behind her. "Are you ready to get up this time?"

Her question implied someone had tried to wake me up before without success. "Maybe."

"You bit your father fairly hard the last time he tried to get you up."

"He probably deserved it."

"While I agree with you, he's sulking."

"Did you marry a child?" I considered burrowing under

the duvet and refusing to emerge for a few years. "What did he want?"

"To feed you. He's anxious. The CDC rep who came to check your virus levels reported the same levels as your last test. Since we have photographic evidence you shifted and an angel's word on it, they're itching to figure out how it's possible you shifted on an underdeveloped virus. The worrywarts out there are going to make themselves sick at the rate they're going. Your male is going to throw up on someone if he doesn't calm his lanky ass down."

"Kenneth?"

"Yes, that male. He's blaming himself for everything, as he'd done so much theater touring looking for you and hadn't realized he was being stalked by that addict he'd busted."

"Good stalkers don't let their victims know, and she had the right ability to do it undetected," I pointed out.

"I wish you the best of luck convincing him of that. We've been trying all morning. His sister's about ready to murder him because he's being stubborn. The living room is a war zone. Spare us from their idiocy, please."

"You want me to get out of bed and tell a bunch of adults to grow up? Before breakfast."

"You also need to have your virus levels checked again, and the CDC rep is here, but after you went for your dad's throat like he was on the menu, no one wants to test their luck."

I wondered how long it would take someone other than me to realize that there was nothing wrong with my virus; they just weren't looking in the right place for it. "I think you're exaggerating."

Mom pointed at the floor, and I rolled over for a look. A

pink, shimmering spot in the pale carpeting betrayed where someone had done decontamination work. "That little spot cost your father five hundred dollars, young lady."

"Serves him right for disturbing me."

"Please just get out of bed, get dressed, and calm the men down already. Your father's sulking, and your male is going to need to be peeled off the ceiling given ten minutes and any stimulation."

"First, I don't have a male. Second, the man that is not my property has a name. It's Kenneth. Third, I do not want to know what a succubus considers to be stimulation."

"Nothing I would find amusing, I assure you. The CDC rep knocked on the door, Emma. He almost went into orbit."

"Maybe you should ask the CDC rep for some pixie dust or a sedative." I stretched, groaned, and considered if I wanted to take a shower before dealing with the disaster in the living room. "Why is Kenneth so jumpy?"

"You're fresh off your first shift, he wants you, and he's afraid he can't compete with every other unmated lycanthrope on the block. I realize you haven't had breakfast yet, but don't be dense. Your father has been warning you about this since you were little. Until you're mated, men are going to be interested in you. Add in your succubus genes, and you're going to be the most interesting woman they've ever seen, and you'll attract women, too. Once your virus has established its claim on your mate, you'll find things are easier. In him, it'll drive other females away from your territory, and it'll keep males away from you, too."

I waved her off. "Yes, yes. I've heard it before. The lycanthropy virus ensures mated couples stick together to procreate, raise children, and spread the virus."

"And your virus is going to be pressuring you to get busy. Either pick, or your virus will pick for you."

"Between you and Ma, you'd have me at the bridal shop picking a dress by the end of the day."

"That might be fun. Do you have anything planned for today?"

"I was planning on starting with killing my father."

"We said we would negotiate!" Kenneth barked from the other room.

"Come tell that to my face you peacock of an FBI agent!" I screamed back.

Mom arched a brow. "Wouldn't you prefer to get dressed first?"

I rolled out of bed, snarled a few curses at my mother, and stomped to the bathroom. While tempted to slam the door, I didn't. Maybe a shower would help. Showers always helped.

THE SHOWER DIDN'T HELP, but at least I was clean and clothed. I wrapped my hair in a towel, piled the mess on my head, and braved the living room, muttering curses over having been woken up so I could be poked and prodded by a CDC rep.

There were a lot more people than I expected in the suite, which soured my mood further. Three men in lab coats stood near the door, probably praying for salvation and a quick escape. Kenneth, his sister, and an older gentleman played cards on the floor, while Dad and Mom took over the couch. "It's just a party in here, isn't it? Where's Ma? What happened to this being a room for two?"

"Please forgive my daughter. By nature, swans are cranky and aggressive. I'm sure she'll settle down after she's picked a mate for herself and marked her territory," Dad said, patting the empty spot on the couch between him and Mom. "Come sit, Emma. Your ma's running some errands. She thought people might relax a bit if she wandered off for a while. There are three CDC reps here to look over your numbers. They brought every meter they could get a hold of trying to figure out why your virus levels are so low for someone capable of shifting."

That explained the three men in lab coats praying for salvation near the door. I pointed at the older man with Kenneth and Jolene. "Who's he?"

"Your future boss, Mr. Weston Harold," my father introduced.

I scowled at Kenneth. "Why haven't we negotiated about the brutal murder of my father yet?"

"You were sleeping," he replied without looking up from his cards. "He even flew in from New York to meet you and sign all the papers so you can start training. We're officially off the case, and we'll need to go through a gauntlet of questioning. Sorry, jail bird. We'll probably be stuck in Colorado for an extra week because of it. In good news, if you can rein that temper in of yours, we can catch the tail end of the retreat and get some dancing in. They revamped the entire schedule. We can slide in whenever we want, although understandably, a lot of the dancers are concerned about additional foul play."

"Can they schedule our questioning for after our dancing?"

Kenneth glanced at his boss, potentially my future boss if I continued to abandon my common sense, and waited.

"I'm sure arrangements can be made," Mr. Harold conceded. "There's the matter of your employment. Fortunately, the FBI doesn't discriminate against lycanthropes, although we will need to do evaluations of your temperament prior to the first training session. Agent Bernard would accompany you, as we've come to the conclusion it's unwise to separate partners even when one is going through training and the other isn't, so he'll get to enjoy another round of training before returning to duty. I would've liked a better chance to evaluate your performance, but I'm satisfied you have the capacity to determine when lethal force is a requirement and have the ability to think on your feet."

"You have an asinine hiring method, Mr. Harold."

"I'm all about the results, and having worked with lycanthropes before, I'm expecting good things from you. Most of the lycanthropes I've worked with have been wolves, so I'll be interested in seeing how an avian works out. You have the education. You're capable of taking care of yourself to an acceptable degree, although I'm going to take Agent Bernard's recommendation for self-defense courses seriously. I'm confident you'll partner well with Agent Bernard, who is notoriously difficult to find a partner for."

"Which defect is responsible for that?"

"We'd be here all day if we made a list. For the sake of efficiency, we'll call it a personality defect coupled with a severe ego. I'm sure you'll have no problems keeping him in line."

I placed my hands on my hips. "We're like fire and gasoline, Mr. Harold."

"That's what makes it fun for both of you. I can promise you one thing: you'll never be bored."

Not being bored went into the pro category, but I

wouldn't admit that to anyone. "I'm going to need a hiring bonus if I'm going to have to put up with him long-term."

"How about a month of paid vacation before you begin training?" he replied.

A month would give me enough time to get my affairs in order before taking an unexpected left turn into law enforcement. "I still think your hiring methods are asinine. I also think you're crazy to want to hire me."

"Honesty is a virtue, although I'd appreciate if you learned some diplomacy when delivering the truth in future."

I shrugged and leveled a glare at Kenneth. "This is all your fault."

Once again, he kept his gaze locked on his cards. "Whatever you say, Little Miss Lawyer."

He annoyed me and my virus in equal measure, resulting in a plume of shed feathers. I flapped over the table and beat the insufferable FBI agent with my wings until Dad pulled me off, restraining me with an iron-hard grip on my neck.

"It's going to be a long day," Dad predicted.

Despite the pummeling I'd given him, Kenneth laughed.

OF THE CDC'S SCANNERS, only one reported a high presence of the virus in my body, giving credence to the theory my virus was hiding out in unconventional places in my body. Once their specialized scanner picked up on the higher concentration of the virus, the three men made progress.

According to their machine, I had a particularly high concentration of virus cells in limited locations, including my brain, the larger bones in my body, and in my torso. Due to the lack of the virus in my bloodstream, they theorized the virus had taken up residence in my digestive and reproduction systems to avoid detection.

"Good for avoiding accidental infection, bad for..." Dad blinked. "Wait, where did you say her virus is accumulating?"

"Her reproductive system, her digestive system, and in her brain, sir," the tech repeated.

"Which means the information on her card about her partner needing to put in a week of serious effort to contract her virus is incorrect, right?"

I honked at my father for daring to speak openly about my non-existent sex life.

"If our reading of this meter is correct, she's highly contagious and should avoid intercourse of all types unless her partner consents to become her mate. Once she shifts back to human, I'd like to take a mouth swab for testing, too. With such a high concentration of the virus in her head, I'm concerned her saliva may contain enough of the virus to be an infection risk."

Dad worked his arm beneath me and carried me to the bathroom. "Kenneth, bring her clothes, please. I'll get her to shift and we'll do a test. You can get a new card issued for her today?"

"Of course, sir. We'll need to update her license as well."

"Her license has a note to check the card already."

"That should be fine as a temporary measure."

After Kenneth left my clothes in the bathroom, Dad dropped a bathrobe over my head. "Try to shift again, please don't attack me, and get dressed. I'll be right outside the door if you need me, so just give a honk. Take a chill pill, and if you want everyone to leave so you can have some private time with Kenneth, just ask us to leave after we do the swab test to see if your saliva has a high concentration of the virus in it."

I wiggled out from beneath the bathrobe and glared at my father.

"If you're not out within five minutes, we're going to assume you're taking a nap again and will come in and fetch you. No diddle-dawdling."

As Dad would do exactly as threatened, I waited for him to leave and close the door behind him before trying his advice again to figure out what actually made me human. The shift happened, and the flash of pain was so intense I curled on the floor and struggled not to cry. I lost several precious minutes struggling to catch my breath before scrambling into the bathrobe because pulling on my jeans seemed too hard when my body still protested the transformation from oversized waterfowl to human.

Living up to his threat, Dad barged in, took a look at me, and sighed. He crouched beside me and wiped my cheeks with the balls of his thumbs. "It hurts less with practice, I promise. Go on, let them test your saliva, and I'll herd the rest of the busybodies out of your space so you can have something to eat and talk to Kenneth for a while. Of course, with the way your virus is yanking you around right now, I expect you two won't be talking."

I flushed. "Dad," I hissed.

He shook his head, stared at the ceiling, and sighed. "You're part succubus, Emma. There's nothing to be embarrassed about."

No matter what I said, I'd lose, so I gave up, tied the robe firmly closed, and wobbled to my feet so the CDC reps could poke and prod at me some more.

A smug Kenneth sat on the couch with a cup of coffee, and he saluted me with it. "Nice outfit."

Dad steered me towards the reps. "Please check her saliva before those two start up again. The sooner we evacuate out of here, the sooner we can call you back to see if she managed to infect the idiot trying his best to provoke her."

My mother laughed. "He's not trying to provoke her. He's successfully provoking her. The instant we leave the room, she's going to pounce him. If you don't want to be pounced, Kenneth, you should leave."

Kenneth's sister joined in the laughter. "Someone has to have handcuffs around here. We can tie him down so he can't escape. That would serve the jerk right for causing so much trouble."

"What happened wasn't his fault," I blurted.

"Emma, eyes away from Kenneth's sister," Dad ordered.

Confused, I stared at him. "What?"

"She's his sister, so she's not infringing on your territory or threatening him."

"I know that!"

"You might, but you're eyeing her like you're considering if you want to go for the throat. I remember that look quite well. You used it on me right before you went for my throat."

Sometimes, I truly and unconditionally hated my father. "She isn't the one who tried to wake me up. That's all on you, Dad."

Jolene hopped to her feet. "And that's my cue to leave my brother to his fate. I'll resume hiding in my room if anyone needs me. Unless I have to plan my brother's funeral, please don't need me."

Kenneth raised a brow. "Good to know you care, Jolene."

"You're a big boy. I'm sure you can handle one single,

cranky female lycanthrope on your own. I'll make sure to tell Mom and Dad you're spending the rest of the week trying your best to catch a contagious disease destined to lead to marriage."

"If you tell them to contact Mr. Sansaul, they might tear into him and not you," Kenneth offered. "As for the rest of it, sure. That works. My phone will be off, as I'll be busy trying to convince her to go with the idea. When I'm not doing that, we'll be dancing, and I might start wanting to kill people if we don't get to do any dancing."

"Good idea about Mr. Sansaul. He might survive their wrath. I still haven't told them I let some bitch get the jump on me yet. I've survived one close brush with death this week. It's your turn. Try not to kill him, Emma. You need him for your nefarious plans. I'd also avoid beating him too hard, no matter how much he deserves it. Too many bruises will interfere with his performance." After blowing her brother a kiss, Jolene bounced out the door.

One of the CDC reps held out a meter, which had a metal attachment sticking out of it. "If you spit on that, it'll take a few seconds to see if your saliva is a contagion source."

Spitting on a metal stick seemed like one of the saner things I'd done over the past few days, so I did as told. The meter remained quiet, and he pressed a few buttons on the display. "Your levels are below threshold for infection," he reported. "We'll want to continue doing quarterly tests to confirm your blood isn't a contagion source, but this is potentially a very advantageous situation for you, Miss Sansaul."

Huh. I'd gotten lucky for once in my life. "Cool. So, I won't be a research subject?"

He laughed. "I wouldn't count on that. The CDC would

love to find out why your virus is replicating in a rather unique way. If it's something that can be replicated, it would make life a lot easier for others with the infection."

"Non-invasive tests when I don't have work would be acceptable."

"And you'll be offered compensation. I'll pass word along and have someone send you a questionnaire about some testing. Have yourself a nice day and try not to destroy the hotel with your enthusiasm. We'll leave some neutralizer here in case you need it." The three techs gathered their meters, packed them away, and bailed.

I found their hurry to get out of the room amusing.

"All right, little chick. We're going to leave you two to your business. Get something to eat and get some dancing in before you really do kill someone. If you need anything, give one of us a call. Mr. Harold? You can worry about paperwork later. Let the love birds have a chance to settle down. Once her virus is satisfied she's not going to lose her male to some interloping female, she should calm enough she can sign papers without her thought process being compromised."

"Sounds good. I'll add the extra paperwork to make her pay effective from when I assigned them to the case to simplify matters on her end. I'm looking forward to discussing this with you more thoroughly, Miss Sansaul."

What had I gotten myself into? "All right, Mr. Harold."

"I'll see you to the lobby," my father said, snagging Mom by the back of her neck and dragging her along. "No helping them, Louisa."

"Why must you insist on ruining my fun, George?"

"Because you're a succubus, and if I let you do exactly what you wanted, you'd turn the resort into a sex party?"

"I still don't see why you think this is a bad thing."

"I'd say I'm monogamous, but I lost that right when I decided marrying an angel was a good idea. Angels come prepackaged with demons, or so I've learned."

"Admit it, George. You like the challenge of trying to wrangle two women."

"I don't get to do any of the wrangling. I'm the one who is wrangled, and you two expect me to like it."

I wondered what it was like to have normal parents. "Please leave without destroying anything or turning the resort into a sex party."

That my parents listened to me shocked me into silence, leaving Kenneth to close and lock the door. "That you need to specify they shouldn't destroy anything or trigger any unscheduled orgies is a little concerning, jail bird."

"Yet you've been given full disclosure of the consequences of sharing space with me."

"You're worth it."

"We hardly know each other!"

"At the risk of sounding like a stalker, I've watched as many of your performances as possible. I bribed your boss to send me a text when you'd be on stage, and he made sure I got a ticket. You're one of the hardest working women I've ever met. Admittedly, I should've looked a little closer, then I would've found your law license and noticed who your father is, but I like to think that makes me a little less creepy. Every time we've run into each other, it's always been the same. I've wanted to learn more about you and do what I could to ruffle your feathers."

"You are aware you drive me crazy, right?"

"That's half the fun. As our boss said, we'll never get bored. I don't want some delicate trophy wife, jail bird. In that, I guess I'm a lot like your father. I need a challenge. You do, too, or else you wouldn't thrive dancing like you do. Anything worth having is worth working for, and I'd rather go in knowing it's going to be hard than expecting it to be easy and learning differently down the road. Making a relationship work takes a lot of effort and dedication on both our parts. The only thing that'll be easy for us is the virus ensuring we need to make it work. I've heard the disclosure so many times today I have it memorized."

"There's no turning back, not even for a succubus."

"I noticed that. I seriously hadn't known the lycanthropy virus could influence a demoness, but sure enough, your mom walks the straight and narrow, doesn't she?"

"Ma helps with that, but yeah. It's hard on her sometimes. If Dad has a bad week at work, she can't feed off him at all. I've seen Ma drag Mom out for a night on the town just so they could have coffee near a brothel so she wouldn't start losing weight."

"That's the last thing I'd ever expected to hear anyone say. Your ma, the angel, took your mom, the succubus, to coffee shops near brothels so she could..."

I laughed at the way Kenneth's expression went blank. "Yes, they'd go hang out near where people were having sex because Dad's lycanthropy virus might be overextended if she tried to get energy from him."

"You have a very strange family life, jail bird. I can promise you a nice, quiet apartment in a good part of town, spacious enough for two to live comfortably, in a secure building. They've even got anti-teleportation wards in place to prevent unwanted pests from arriving unannounced."

"Those wards can block angels?"

"An archangel can get through it, as can greater devils,

but frankly, if one of those shows up, we have more to worry about than some busted anti-teleportation wards. I like living in a high security building as I don't want my work following me home."

After what had happened with Cathy, I understood all too well. "You have a very tempting sales pitch, Agent Bernard."

"We'll also get to spend your ma's money, as I had accepted her dowry offer and insisted on a pay increase to make sure you're well fed. You're cranky when you're hungry. Now that they're gone, I thought I'd order something so we wouldn't have to leave the room and put some innocent server at risk of becoming your next meal."

I flushed. "I'm so sorry I beat you with my wings. Did I hurt you?"

"Not at all. I bet you could inflict a lot of damage with those wings of yours if you wanted, but you didn't hit me hard. Thank you for not pecking me with that beak of yours, though. It's like you have a knife attached to your face."

"Dad can poke a hole through someone's throat with his if he really wants."

"That's both terrifying and comforting."

"Comforting? How so?"

"If anyone tries to hurt you, I know you can shift and poke holes in their throat. I find that very comforting."

"Now you sound like my father."

"That's because a good man doesn't need a contagious disease to want his woman capable of kicking the asses of anyone who might hurt her. I meant it. First thing we're doing when we get back to New York is enrolling you in self-defense courses, and I'll attend lessons with you. I'll also take you to the gun range and start your lessons on handling firearms before FBI training so you won't have to scramble as much to catch up. A month of self-defense and firearms training should be enough time to get you up to speed on the basics and get you used to handling a firearm."

I had the feeling Kenneth had put a lot of thought into the near future, and I recognized he indulged in his protective instincts. When Dad worried about Ma or Mom, he did similar things, although my mothers rarely needed any help handling their problems.

Sometimes, I felt bad for my father, who had no chance in hell of coming out on top with an angel and a demoness around.

Still, my odd family worked, and I had no shame in wanting a man who'd try to fill the same roles my father did for both my mothers. I gave it a week before Kenneth drove me mad trying, which was the approximate frequency of incidents in my household. However much I was my father's daughter, I had an equal blend of my mothers in me, which spelled trouble for Kenneth in all ways.

"I get pissy when I can't dance, so I'm going to need at least an hour a day or someone might get hurt," I warned.

"As I enjoy dancing, too, I have no problems with this arrangement, although I hope you'll indulge in some swing dancing rather than prancing around on our toes all day. I watch ballerinas and get calf cramps trying to figure out how you do that throughout an entire performance."

"Pain, suffering, dedication, and blood," I replied.

Being infected with lycanthropy made the bleeding part problematic, although I'd learned to be aware of when I developed blisters and sores as a result of working too hard for my own good.

"We're going to have to work on the bleeding part of that."

"It doesn't happen often, and nowadays, I heal almost as fast as they develop. It's a useful side effect of being a lycanthrope."

"I can work with that. Any other demands?"

"I tend to be inflexible about my budget, and when I overspend, the first thing I dip into is my food budget," I confessed. "I'll be eating noodles for the next month making up for this trip."

"Not in my apartment you won't. The food budget is officially my problem. You can be a stickler for the rest of the finances, but I refuse to let you starve yourself because you wanted a little luxury. Non-negotiable. I'm spoiled, and if I have to eat noodles for a month, I'll kill somebody."

Laughing, I shook my head. "You already have me moving into your apartment?"

"Damn straight I already have you moving into my apartment. It's my current mission to rescue you from that triad of insanity you call your parents. Trust me on this one, jail bird. I've seen my mother prowl after my father wanting another baby. Heaven help anyone who gets in the way of a woman on a mission to have another baby. My poor father never stood a chance. Your dad? He's got two women hunting him. I'm doing all of you a favor. If I don't take you, your mothers might sell you to the highest bidder so they can have another baby."

As both of my mothers could be ruthless in entirely different ways, I worried he was right. "It seems I honk in my sleep."

"Small price to pay to have my very own swancubus."

"Swancubus? Really?"

"Part swan, part succubus, all mine."

"What about the angel? I'm part angel, too."

"Swangecubus doesn't sound as nice. Neither does angswancubus. Swancubus has a nice ring to it."

"Has anyone ever told you you're a bit weird?"

"From time to time. That's also funny coming from a woman with two mothers."

"Point," I conceded. "Why me? Why not some other woman?"

"I don't want some other woman. I want you. You caught my attention when you snorted pixie dust of all things, but after that? Every time I saw you, you were working so hard to make something of yourself without caring what others thought of you. To this day, I've never been able to figure out why you'd even want to use pixie dust in the first place."

"It's all Mom's fault. She promised I'd have a good time and it wouldn't hurt anything, and Mom's a prankster, but she wouldn't hurt me. On purpose, at least."

"You know what I think?"

I narrowed my eyes. "What do you think?"

"I think you have a nosy ma who'd peeked into her daughter's future to see who was in store for her. And since you've proven to be the type who needs to be kicked out of the nest, she told your mom what I looked like and set up an elaborate scheme to ensure we met. Then, those two played the long game."

Mom would pull such a stunt without hesitation, and I'd seen Ma cheat enough times to know she would, too. Together, the pair terrified me, and I had no doubt they'd concoct a scheme to ensure I'd leave home one day. "They would. Those insufferable..." I choked back a scream of frustration and pulled my hair. "They would! They really would."

"And it would explain why your ma was so willing to offer a dowry, too."

"May I please borrow your phone a minute?"

"Of course." Kenneth retrieved it from the coffee table and handed it to me.

I dialed Ma's number from memory and connected the call.

"I see you've stolen Agent Bernard's phone again," Ma answered.

"I want the truth, nothing but the truth, and the whole truth, you feathered menace from hell!" I howled.

"It seems your father was not exaggerating that you're in a rather miffed mood today. What do you want to know?"

"Did you and Mom conspire to get me high on pixie dust so I'd meet Kenneth?"

Ma's sweet laughter rang out. "Would I, a sweet, innocent angel, do such a thing to my own daughter?"

"Yes, you would. Without hesitation."

"You've answered your own question, my sweet child. Do enjoy your week with him, and as I am such a sweet, loving angel, I asked Louisa to make sure you wouldn't grace us with a grandchild quite yet. Enjoy your mate's company for the next week, and as soon as you get back to New York, have him look into birth control if you don't want any little ones under foot quite yet. It's a known problem for female lycanthropes to have trouble with their birth control. Enjoy yourself, Emma."

Ma hung up on me, and I gaped at the darkened display of Kenneth's phone.

"I'm going to hazard a guess she said something you didn't expect."

"She confirmed your theory is accurate. She also coerced

Mom into fiddling with me so I can't have children for the next week, and she wants me to tell you you need to get birth control next week because it won't work for me."

Kenneth covered his mouth with his hand and cleared his throat. "So, you're telling me we have all week to ensure I contract your virus without having to worry about children?"

Some days, I loved my parents, but others, I wanted to kill all three of them for putting me into awkward situations. Some days, like today, they managed to do both. "That's exactly what I'm telling you."

"Is sending them flowers and a thank you card the appropriate response for this? Because seriously? Men dream about the day they win a beautiful woman and earn the permission of both parents. In your case, I have three parents to worry about, and one's a lycanthrope, which means he can pop my head off at his leisure."

Poor Kenneth. When I thought about it that way, he had a lot more to lose than I did, including his head. "I'd offer to protect you, but honestly, I have a really bad track record at protecting men from my father. After the first half dozen or so times a wolf came calling and Dad beat him up, I stopped trying."

"I'd say I could handle myself around your father fine, but I'm going to hide behind you if I ever make him angry. He probably won't go through you to get to me."

The only way I could protect Kenneth from my father was to claim him as my mate, as lycanthropes were documented to spend an obscene amount of time grieving over a lost partner, which would ensure he wouldn't get any of the grandchildren I knew Dad ultimately desired. Lycanthropes were so predictable and easy to manipulate. "If he wants grandchildren, he won't touch you, and he knows it."

"I like that train of thought, and I especially like how determined you sound. Do you think you'll need a full week to stake your claim, or is that sneaky little virus of yours robust enough to take what it wants right out of the gate?"

Kenneth Bernard was a little bit of heaven and a little bit of hell mixed together to drive me wild, but some mistakes were worth making. I had no real reason to say no, and when I thought about it, I had more reasons than I cared to count to say yes.

Somehow, we'd make it work. It'd probably be a glorious mess, just like the odd relationship between my father and mothers so often was, but we'd get through it somehow.

"Let's find out."

He needed no other invitation.

The next novel in the Magical Romantic Comedy (with a body count) series is Blending In. These stories can, with the exception of Burn, Baby, Burn (sequel to Playing with Fire,) be read in any order.

About R.J. Blain

RJ BLAIN suffers from a Moleskine journal obsession, a pen fixation, and a terrible tendency to pun without warning.

When she isn't playing pretend, she likes to think she's a cartographer and a sumi-e painter.

In her spare time, she daydreams about being a spy. Should that fail, her contingency plan involves tying her best of enemies to spinning wheels and quoting James Bond villains until she is satisfied.

RJ also writes as Susan Copperfield, Bernadette Franklin, Audrey Greene, G.P. Robbins, and Lilith Daniels. Visit RJ and her pets (the Management) at thesneakykittycritic.com.

FOLLOW RJ & HER ALTER EGOS ON BOOKBUB:
RJ BLAIN
SUSAN COPPERFIELD
BERNADETTE FRANKLIN
G.P. ROBBINS

Audrey Greene
Lilith Daniels